# SACRIFICE OF THE BRAVE KING

## THE POSEIDON TRIALS

ELIZA RAINE

Editors: Hart to Heart Edits

*You're not broken.*
*You just haven't found what brings you to life yet...*

# ALMI

*I* tugged at the bedroom door. It was still locked.

I was alone and shaking, tears streaming down my face.

I had never felt so helpless.

"Why?" I yelled at the locked door. "Why are you doing this?"

I didn't know if I was raging at Poseidon or Atlas.

At that point, I fucking hated them both.

Things had finally been going well. *Better* than well. We had gotten ahead in the Trials, my magic getting stronger, our foes easier to beat. We had a very real chance of winning.

My magic growing was increasing our chances of finding the Heart of the Ocean — which meant I was getting closer to saving Lily.

And then... Then Atlas took her.

I picked up the nearest thing to me — a glass of water on the stand inside the door — and hurled it at the wall with another bellow of rage. "Fucking asshole," I screamed.

I had done nothing to him. Lily had done nothing to him.

And Poseidon... I had been starting to believe he was far more to me than an ally. But then he had sent me away. Again.

How could he? I had as much power as he did, who the fuck did he think he was to decide it was too dangerous for me?

I might have been able to talk Atlas around, or my air magic might have smashed them to pieces — there might have been a hundred ways I could have gotten Lily back. But Poseidon didn't trust me. He didn't respect me.

He just fucking sent me away.

My eyes burned as furious tears kept coming, and I looked around for something to hurl.

He had betrayed me.

Atlas may have taken my sister—and fury filled me at the thought—but Poseidon had brought me as close to him as I had ever been to anyone and then betrayed my trust. He had treated me like a child, a weakling; useless. I was used to feeling fury. But betrayal was new.

"Asshole!" I launched the entire wooden stand at the wall. A leg snapped off as it made contact, before clattering to the ground.

A small squeak reached my ears over the rush of pounding blood.

"Kryvo?"

"Almi." He sounded terrified, and a tiny bit of my rage melted away. Enough for me to hurry over to the dresser. "Please don't throw anything in my direction," he whispered.

"I'm sorry." My voice broke on the word, and my angry tears were replaced by a heaving sob that took me by surprise.

"What happened?" he asked, his voice still tiny.

I slumped onto the stool at the dresser, lifting him carefully from his cushion. I suddenly craved his warmth and the feeling of not being alone so hard I could have kissed the little starfish. I set him on my palm, and his suckers hooked in.

"Atlas killed Silos and took my sister," I choked.

"What? Why? How?"

"Poseidon was having Silos watched, and he and everyone in the bakery had been turned to stone by the time we got there, and Lily was gone." Never-ending tears rolled down my face and I swiped at them. "And then Atlas showed up, and said he had taken Lily. He tried to get Poseidon to forfeit the Trials in return for giving her back, and when Poseidon said no, Atlas said he had no need for me anymore. He said his wife was coming, and I think he meant to kill me. He said his wife had my sister with her. But before she got there Poseidon flashed me here."

Kryvo said nothing a moment, then spoke. "I need more details. Tell me again. Slowly."

"I can't! I need to get back there, to get Lily!"

"Why did Poseidon flash you away?"

"He said it was too dangerous for me to be there, but

he can barely use his magic! Persephone said the poison weakened him, and—" I banged my fist on the dresser as emotion overwhelmed me.

I was scared for Poseidon, I realized angrily.

I didn't want to be scared for him! I wanted to hate him. But the truth was, Atlas could kill him. Easily. And the thought of that was so intolerable that fresh emotion surged up inside me.

"He has Galatea with him," I said, trying to take a calming breath. "She is strong. He's not alone."

"Almi… There may be a good reason he sent you away."

My memory flashed on the green hand pushing through Galatea's shield, and I shuddered.

"I have to get back there. Now. I have to help. I have to get my sister back."

A voice suddenly boomed through my room, reverberating through the walls. "Your sister is safe. I will return to the palace as soon as I can."

"Poseidon?" I stared up at the walls, momentarily stunned. "Poseidon!" I yelled again. "Tell me what the fuck is happening!"

Nothing but silence answered me. My tears had stopped, though.

*He was safe. And Lily was safe.*

Nothing was more important than that.

"Where is he? Why the hell isn't he back here right now? I need to know what's happening!" I stood up, restless energy and adrenaline coursing through me. I kicked at the foot of the bed as I tried to swallow down my anger and failed.

"For once I wish he'd just fucking answer my questions, instead of being so cryptic and mysterious and pigheaded and—"

Kryvo cut my tirade off. "We could get answers ourselves."

"What?"

"This is probably a bad idea, but… He told you there was more of the prophecy."

"Yes."

"After you, erm, sent me away," he said, awkwardly, "did he tell you any more?"

"No."

"I have been searching the palace for anything about the Heart of the Ocean, and I can find nothing. I think…" He took a small pause. "I think we should go and see the Oracle."

I blinked. "Poseidon said he would take me to the Oracle, once the Trials were over. And… And Atlas said something about her." I sifted through my blurry memories of what had just happened. "He said he had been to see her, and that I was under-informed."

"I think we should take advantage of Poseidon not being here. I think you need to know everything you can about yourself, and how you are connected to the blight. Look at your shell."

I turned to the mirror and sucked in a breath. The green color was seeping into yellow, tinged with orange at the edges. The shell was three-quarters filled with color.

I bit down on my lip as I wiped the drying tears from my cheeks.

I had so many questions that Poseidon wouldn't

5

answer. He had just shown me how little he trusted me, how little respect he had for me. Why should I trust him to decide what I should and shouldn't know about my own destiny?

The green hand pushing through the water flashed into my head again, the image becoming hard to shift. Had that been Atlas' wife?

"Will the Oracle tell me what Poseidon did to Atlas' wife?"

"She might, if it is relevant. We need to go before Poseidon comes back."

"We're locked in. I don't know how to get out."

"We know a goddess who might help us," he said.

I lifted him to my face. "Kryvo, you're a fucking genius."

He flushed hot on my hand, before I set him back down on his cushion and ran to where my belt was slung on an armchair.

I rummaged through the pouches until I produced Persephone's gold rose. I clutched it tight, closed my eyes, and spoke aloud.

"Persephone, I hope you can hear me. I need your help."

The smell of the forest washed over me, and when my eyelids fluttered open, Persephone stood before me.

"Thank you, thank you, thank you for coming," I said in a rush.

"What's happening? Are you okay?"

"No. I'm not. Poseidon has locked me in here, *'for my own safety'*, and I'm done putting up with his bullshit."

Persephone cocked her head at me. Her slight build was clad in black jeans and a yellow blouse, her white hair tied up in a big messy bun on top of head. "You looked like you were getting on pretty well, last time I saw you."

"Well, that was before."

"Before what?"

I took a breath, then told her everything, as compactly as I could. "I just need you to get me to the stables. From there, I can get Blue and manage on my own."

She snorted at me, folding her arms. "I don't doubt for minute that you can manage on your own, but I don't think you *should*."

I stared at her. "You won't help me?"

"Of course I will, but I'm coming with you."

"What?"

"Do you know where to find Delphi and the Oracle?"

"No, but I think my starfish does."

She shook her head. "What kind of friend would I be, if I let you go roaming around Apollo's realm, or pissing off Oracles, by yourself? Get that dress off, get some pants on, and let's go, before Poseidon gets here."

# ALMI

*I* hurriedly changed my clothes in the bathroom, nerves thrilling through me.

*The Oracle.*

I was actually going to see the Oracle. The woman I had been blaming, alongside Poseidon, for my sister's condition for years. She was the only person who might have answers. And boy, did I have a lot of questions. So many questions.

Persephone coming with me gave me more comfort than I would ever admit. She had magic, connections, and knowledge. She would make this trip a hundred times easier and give me a real chance of getting there before Poseidon could interfere.

I half jogged out of the bathroom, wearing black woolen pants from the closet, and a shirt over my vest, my tattoo on show. Kryvo was stuck to my shoulder, and I'd braided my increasingly bright blue hair over the other shoulder with little care, just wanting it out of the way. Persephone regarded me briefly.

"You sort of look like a sexy pirate, except those pants are… not so sexy."

"I want answers from the Oracle, not a night of passion with her."

"All the same," Persephone said with a shrug. "Let me see if I can try out a new trick Hecate taught me." She waved her hand at me, a green vine shooting out. As soon as it made contact with my pants, they changed, the woolen material smoothing out and fitting snugly against my thighs.

"You've given me leather pants," I said, staring.

"Yup. You ready to go?"

I nodded, and we flashed.

"Wow."

My mouth fell open as I took in what I was seeing. The temple of Delphi, I assumed. It was white marble, with a triangular roof and Greek style columns, and looked fairly unremarkable, aside from two tall iron dishes at the top of the steps to the entrance, flickering with blue light.

What was remarkable was where the temple was positioned.

The top of a mountain. The *very* top of a mountain.

We were standing on a small marble platform jutting out of the front of the temple, and there were no railings, the smooth stone surface offering nothing in the way of grip. It felt like we were balanced precariously on the tip of the peak, the platform at risk of tipping either way at any point.

The view was dizzying. I didn't know how high up we were, but I could see an entire range of mountains stretching out below and beyond us, all snow-capped and surrounded by pastel-colored Olympus clouds.

"It's beautiful," I breathed, turning in a slow and careful circle.

"No, it's not." Persephone's voice was unsteady, and her face was white when I turned to her.

"You okay?"

"I freaking hate heights," she said, taking a slow backward step toward the temple. I moved to her, taking her shaking arm.

"You can flash to safety if you need to, any time," I said reassuringly.

She nodded. "I know, or my knees would already have given out. This is good for me. Facing my fears and all that."

"You're doing great." Together, we moved carefully to the steps leading inside the temple. As we reached the top of them, a lyrical voice sang out of nowhere.

"Only one may enter."

Persephone looked at me. "Have you got my rose on you?"

"Yes," I nodded.

Relief washed over her face. "Good. I'm leaving. Call me when you want me to come get you."

"I really, really appreciate your help." She had been willing to stay on the top of the mountain and deal with her fear, just for me.

"Be careful," she smiled at me, then disappeared in a

flash. I took one last look at the incredible vista, then headed into the gloom of the temple.

The inside looked nothing like I thought it would. In fact, it looked nothing like I thought anything would.

The walls and ceiling were gold, and in the shining surfaces were scratched hundreds and hundreds of words in languages I couldn't read. Light radiated from the walls, reflecting off the enormous pool that dominated the central area of the temple.

I stared as I came to a stop at the top of a set of stairs leading down to the water. There was a stone platform in the middle of the pool, covered in a bed of cushions and a bowl of fruit. The scent of lavender permeated the air.

The water in front of the platform rippled, drawing my eye. The water looked as golden as the walls, and slowly a figure rose from the liquid. A woman, head shrouded in hessian, dark skin glowing and youthful, and her amber eyes bright.

The Oracle of Delphi.

"Almi." Her voice sounded clear and deep. The water around her rippled, light shimmering in golden rings.

"Hello." I was more nervous than I had expected to be, sweat pricking at my skin.

"I have been expecting you for some time."

"Well, you can see into the future, so..." I shrugged awkwardly.

"Incorrect. I do not see into the future. I am aware of certainties, and I can see links and bonds."

"You told Poseidon he had to marry me."

"Also incorrect. I told the King of the Sea that if he possessed the heart of a nereid, he would also possess the Heart of the Ocean."

"Which meant marrying me."

She raised her shoulders in the slightest of shrugs. "That is how Poseidon chose to interpret the prophecy. Is that what you wish to talk to me about?"

I almost said yes, but shook my head. "No. I have two questions," I said, holding my hand up. The smell of lavender was becoming overpowering. "One, what is the Heart of the Ocean?"

She lifted her arms from the water painfully slowly. Her skin was veined with gold, and more water rippled out around her. "The Heart of the ocean is not a heart at all."

I stared at her. "Right. Want to be any more vague?"

A tiny smile played at her lips. "You do not see what is before you, Queen Almi."

"I'm not a Queen."

"You are."

"Whatever. What is the Heart of the Ocean if it's not a heart?"

"You will find out, soon enough."

I glared at her and she stared back. "Fine," I hissed eventually. I clearly wasn't getting any more from her. "Question two, is there any way to cure the stone blight without the Heart of the Ocean?"

"No."

I growled in frustration. "Are you sure?"

"Yes. You are the only one who may find it."

"How?"

"You are not of the ocean."

"Yeah, I just found that out. I have air magic. But that doesn't answer my question."

"Everything needs air. Fire, water, earth. None exist without each other, and air is at the heart of everything."

"Are you saying my air magic will help get the Heart of the Ocean?"

"Your full power will lead you to it."

Relief washed over me. It was as we had suspected. When my shell tattoo was filled with color and my power fully present, we would be able to find the stupid heart.

"I have answered your two questions. Is there anything else?"

I bit my lip as I considered.

I knew what I wanted to ask her something else, but a tiny bit of me felt I was betraying Poseidon by doing so.

*He sent me away, and he doesn't trust me,* I told myself.

I would regret not asking when I had the chance.

"What was the whole prophecy you gave Poseidon about marrying a Nereid?"

"What do you mean, the whole prophecy?" She tilted her head slowly, the fabric swathing her not moving at all.

"I heard the first bit, about marrying a Nereid. Then something about true love, but it was cut off."

She moved her arms around slowly, expression darkening. "Poseidon has not told you?"

"No. He told me there was more to it than I was aware of, but he wouldn't tell me what it was."

She brought her arms back down, palms flat on the water, and flames fired to life across the back of her hands, spreading across the surface of the pool like oil.

Her eyes turned milky, and the flames leaped high around her, the whole pool on fire. I stepped forward, unsure what to do and my nerves edging on panic, but then she spoke.

"He who possesses the heart of a Nereid shall possess the Heart of the Ocean. True love is not a necessity, pure possession will seal the deal. But be warned. True love will never go unnoticed. Should a Nereid fall in love, she will die, her mortal body cast aside, and her soul made extinct."

I stared at the woman in the flames, her words ringing in my ears. My whole body felt like it had been doused in ice.

*If I fell in love, I'd die?*

"Poseidon knew this?" My words were a mumble, my mouth not working properly.

"He has known a long time."

"He didn't tell me. He didn't tell me I couldn't fall in love."

"You *can* fall in love. But the moment true love is reciprocal, you will die. If you fall for someone who does not love you back, then your body and soul will be safe. Be warned though, unrequited love wreaks havoc on the mind. Not a much better fate than death, I suspect."

I had given up on love years ago. The revelation that falling in love might kill me shouldn't have mattered. But... There was something between Poseidon and I. Something beyond our physical attraction, something that hit me on a level I had never felt before. All I could see in my mind as the Oracle spoke was his face, hard and severe, and those beautiful eyes filled with raw, boundless power.

Did I really believe I might fall in love with him? The god who'd wrecked my life?

I replayed her words again, trying to work them out in my head, trying to understand why thoughts of Poseidon were dominating my reaction to the revelation.

*Should a Nereid fall in love, she will die, her mortal body cast aside, and her soul made extinct.*

Did that mean all Nereids? Or just me?

"Is this the same for all Nereids?" I asked the Oracle aloud.

"You are the only one left."

"No, my sister is alive."

"Lily is neither alive, nor dead, while she sleeps."

"Why is she asleep?" My words came out abrupt and angry, my emotion beginning to creep free of my control. "And what does gods weeping have to do with her?"

"She sleeps to awaken you."

My heart skipped a beat. "What?"

"The closer she moves to death, the farther you move toward power."

"No." I felt the hard stone hit my knees as I dropped to the tiles, my head swimming. "No, that can't be true."

"Everything I say to you is true."

"I'm getting my magic because Lily is dying?"

"Yes."

"No. No, this can't be right." The repercussions of what she was saying hammered through me, and I felt sick. "The only way to cure the stone blight is with the Heart of the Ocean," I whispered.

"Yes."

"And the only way to get that is for me to get my full power."

"Yes."

"Which means…" I trailed off, unable to finish the sentence, my throat closing.

The Oracle finished it for me. "Lily must die to cure the rest of Aquarius — including its King."

# ALMI

For a moment, I couldn't breathe. My throat was closing completely, and I couldn't get any air into my darkening mind.

The implications of what the woman in the pool before me had just said were too much for me to process, too huge for me to make sense of.

To save Poseidon and all those people, my sister had to die. And it would be me who killed her. My magic.

As if on cue, my throat opened as though it were being forced, air rushing into my body.

I gasped as I realized it was my air magic, trying to help me. I looked down at the shell on my chest, two-thirds filled with color.

Anger bordering on rage gushed trough my body. "No!"

"I am sorry."

I snapped my eyes from my tattoo to the Oracle. "Bullshit! Nobody is fucking sorry! Nobody! You, Poseidon,

Atlas — you're all just playing some fucked-up game, and the person who loses is my sister!"

The rage had broken free, and I was vaguely aware of my hair whipping around my face, my shirt blowing against my skin, and my legs straightening, lifting me from my knees.

"Why? Why does she have to pay?" *And why did I have to be the one who would kill her?*

A sob tore from my throat. The flames around the Oracle rose higher. "Fate. You are bound to the life you are living."

"No! I am free! I make my own decisions!" I knew even as I yelled the words they were futile. I hadn't been in control of my life for even a moment of it. Control was an illusion.

"You do not."

"What if I refuse? What if I don't want this stupid fucking magic?" The air whipping around me fell away in an instant. An uncomfortable feeling of danger swirled through my anger.

"If you refuse your magic, in order to keep your sister alive, then you will never find the Heart of the Ocean."

"And Poseidon will die?"

The Oracle nodded. "Along with the citizens of Aquarius affected by the stone blight."

A wave of hopelessness crashed over me, and I pressed my hands to my face, as though I could force some clarity into my overloaded head.

I already knew what Lily would do, what she would say to me if she were there.

There was no way in Olympus that she would put her own life over others. But it wasn't her choice. It was mine.

"There must be another way," I said, removing my hands, desperation in my voice as I stared at the Oracle. "There has to be. What about Atlantis?"

The Oracle tilted her head slowly. "What do you know of Atlantis?"

"It has a font that can heal anything. Can it heal Lily?"

"The Font of Zoi is the reason you are in this position now."

"What?"

"Almi." The deep male voice saying my name didn't belong to the Oracle. I focused my gaze over her shoulder, my eyes landing on Poseidon.

My breath caught again, more black dots invading my vision as emotion threatened to overwhelm me. He was covered in stone. Hardly any patches of his warm, tanned skin showed at all as he stepped to the side of the pool, moving stiffly toward me.

"You should have told me." I couldn't help the words leaving my mouth. He glanced at the Oracle, then back to me.

"Told you what?"

"All of it."

"All of the prophecy?" He was speaking gently, as though I were a bomb he was scared of setting off.

"Yes. All of the prophecy. And about Lily."

His expression darkened, and he frowned. "What of Lily?" he asked carefully.

"She is dying because of me."

He was close enough now that I could see the emotion

in his face when he reacted. Surprise. And sadness. *He hadn't known.*

"She is safe now," he said.

He hadn't known that my power was killing her. And he had saved her from Atlas.

Tears spilled down my cheeks as my anger with him leaked away. "Where is she?"

"You need to rest."

"Where is she?"

"In the palace. With the others."

"My magic is killing her. When I get it all, she'll die."

He reached out an arm, and his touch was rough and cool. The touch of stone. "I'm sorry."

"You need help," I said, looking down dazedly at his arm.

"Yes. Let me take you home, then I must see the dragon."

I looked from him to the Oracle. "Tell me about Atlantis first," I said.

She gave me a sad smile. "Poseidon can tell you about Atlantis. Once he is healed." She moved her sightless eyes to him, and there was no doubting her words were a command aimed directly at the ocean god.

He nodded slowly. "I will."

When the light from Poseidon's flash cleared, I found myself back in my room and Poseidon gone.

I didn't even check to see if the door was locked. No anger welled up in me this time. Just bone-deep sadness.

I moved to the dresser, lifted Kryvo from my shoulder and onto his cushion. "You okay?" he asked quietly.

"Not really." I made my way to the bed, climbed onto the huge mattress, then fell, face-first onto the pillows. Blessed darkness engulfed my vision, and I let the hot, silent tears come.

I knew what I had to do now.

I had to talk to my sister.

Whether or not the Lily who lived in my head was my own projection or really her made no difference. I needed her. And I needed to tell her how sorry I was.

"Lily?" The fabric around my face muffled my voice, and I was glad. I didn't want to see or hear anything, except her.

*Almi.*

Her hair was as bright blue as I'd ever seen it, her skin glittering and shining with pearly pastels, as she materialized in my head. I let her image fill every part of my mind.

"I'm sorry. I'm so, so sorry."

*I'm not.*

"What?"

*I've always known you were destined for something big, little sister. And I was right. You're going to save the whole damn realm.* Her smile was big and warm. *I'm thrilled.*

"But... I'm killing you."

*Almi, I've not lived any kind of life for nearly a decade. I only wanted to come back for you. Because you wanted me. My purpose was always to help.* Her big blue eyes were filled with sincerity. *How better can I help than to give you what you need to save Aquarius?*

"It's not fair."

*No, it's not.*

"I need you. I need you to come back."

*No, you don't.*

"Yes, I do! I've been trying to get you back forever. I can't give up now!" I punched at the pillows either side of my head.

*You wouldn't be giving up. You would be embracing what you and I were born to do. Between us, we'll save Aquarius. And save the man who loves you.*

I stilled. "Loves me?"

Lily smiled again, this time playfully. *You know, you're very naive, for a woman of your age.*

"Poseidon doesn't love me."

*That is a conversation for you two to have, not one for me to be involved in.*

I lay in the pillows, silent for a moment, tears still streaming into the bedding. "Lily, I can't be the cause of your death. I just… can't."

*You mean you won't.*

"Fine. I won't. I can refuse the magic. I know I can."

*And watch Poseidon die? Watch the families of Aquarius fall to the blight, one by one? Watch what's left of the realm fall to Atlas and his cronies?*

I didn't answer, fear and anger swirling about in my head and mixing into frustration. I could do that no more than I could cause Lily's death, and she knew it.

*Almi, if you don't cure Poseidon of the stone blight soon, then you two will lose the Poseidon Trials. That affects the whole of Olympus. It is no exaggeration to say that the fate of this world lies with you.*

I pushed myself out of the pillows, rolling onto my

back and staring angrily at the ceiling. "I am not equipped to save the fucking world. You just said it yourself, I'm naive. Everyone thinks I'm odd. And I'm on my own."

*You're odd, for sure, but you are most definitely not on your own. You have Kryvo, Galatea, Persephone, and Poseidon. You are surrounded by people who care for you.*

As I thought about it, I started to believe she was right. She wasn't just trying to comfort me. Persephone was my friend. If I hadn't known that before today, I was given proof when she clung to a mountain top for me, despite being terrified. Kryvo constantly faced his own fears to help me. Galatea had started looking at me with respect instead of suspicion, and I was pretty sure she would describe herself as caring for me in her own way. And Poseidon... Poseidon was something else to me. Not a friend. But I was sure he cared for me.

Did he love me?

*Could* he love me?

He'd sent me away to be on my own, unable to help my sister. He couldn't have done that if he loved me.

Shaking my head, I forced the thoughts away. "If I have all these powerful gods and friends around me, then surely there's another way. Poseidon is going to tell me something about Atlantis."

*The Oracle was clear. There's only one way. Please don't get your hopes up.*

"That's a hard habit to break, Lily. I've been getting my hopes up for as long as I can remember."

She chuckled. *And thank the gods for that. You're tenacious. You're a survivor.*

"I'll never be as strong as you are."

*You'll be stronger,* Lily whispered. *I just had boring old water magic. You have something incredible. Air that can merge with water, with fire, with earth. Did you see how your power blended with Poseidon's?*

My mind flicked through memories of the last Trial, and the elation I had felt afterward. And the deepening of the bond with Poseidon, the unspoken connection that had become impossible to suppress.

"Does all magic merge like that?"

*It depends. At the Academy, they told us that certain types of magic could work together, but not usually from two different people. And only under the control of powerful gods.*

"I'm not a god."

*No, but you are married to one. One of the most powerful in Olympus. Brother of Zeus and Hades, King of the Sea.* She grinned. *Ideal husband material.*

I let out a long breath, shaking my head slowly. "I can't lose you, Lily."

*You'll always have your memories.*

"I need more than that. I need to wake you up."

*You need to save the world.*

## POSEIDON

"What did you tell her?"

Fear rolled through me, my limbs, my face, my skin, all starting to feel numb as the stone crawled across my body.

The Oracle stared at me with sightless eyes. "You should have told her yourself."

"You told her the rest of the prophecy. About falling in love being the cause of her death." I felt sick, emotion making me angry.

"She was less concerned with that than learning that she will be the cause of her sister's death."

"Explain."

"Her magic comes at a cost. For her to reach her full potential, her sister must die."

"Then she will refuse the power. She loves her sister more than anything in Olympus." There was no way Almi would be a part of killing her own sister.

The Oracle shook her head. "Then she will not be able

to obtain the Heart of the Ocean. And then you will die. You and all the inhabitants of Aquarius. Atlas will get the revenge he so desperately desires."

Horror coiled in my gut at her words.

This couldn't be. How could Almi have been put in such an impossible position?

"Are you speaking the words of a prophecy, or is this your opinion?" I ground out.

"Lily must die, for Almi to save your life. That is prophecy."

Rage exploded through me, and I felt the stone tighten over my skin, blocking my power form erupting.

"I have vowed to save her sister."

"Then you have vowed to mark your own end. And that of your kingdom."

"Who did this? Why is this happening to her and Lily?"

"Almi has the potential to carry phenomenal power. That must be tempered. Tested. Proven."

"By killing her own sister?"

"By being forced to make a decision for the greater good."

"This is cruelty beyond measure."

"It is life in Olympus. Life wielding enormous power."

"It is hatred and bitterness and resentment."

"Emotions you know much about. Emotions you have caused in abundance in others."

"You are referring to Atlas?"

"You have brought this upon yourself, Sea King. And the unrequited love you feel for your bride? You have done her no favors. Saved her from nothing."

I didn't hear another word from the deity's mouth. My head was spinning, my rage barely under control, and my body succumbing to the stone.

*Hades!* I sent the plea for help to my brother, just as my legs gave out, and blackness swamped me.

# ALMI

*A* gentle knock at my door snapped me from my reverie.

I didn't know how long I'd been sitting on the bed, trying to work out what the hell I was supposed to do next.

I leapt up, hoping it was Poseidon come to tell me about Atlantis, but already knowing from the knock that it wasn't him. It had been too soft.

I pulled the door open and saw Persephone. "Hi." She looked me up and down and frowned. "You look terrible."

"I feel terrible."

She nodded, as though making up her mind. "We'll go to my place. I've got some stuff that will make you feel better."

I looked at her, and my concern must have been evident, because she reached her hands up, gently clasping my shoulders. "Medicine. Maybe some wine. Nothing weird."

"Is it a bit early for wine?" I realized I didn't even know what time of day it was.

"It's never too early for wine. Also, no. It's the middle of the night."

I nodded, dazedly, then stopped. "I can't. I have to wait for Poseidon. The Oracle said he had to tell me something important."

Persephone's expression tightened, and alarm shot through me. "That's sort of why I came. Hades had to take him to the dragon again. She's a miserable dragon in the first place, and now she's being really grumpy."

"What happened?" Fear for Poseidon, unwanted but fierce, slammed through me.

"He's not in a good way. She's only been able to get rid of some of the stone this time, and she told Hades she won't help him again, because it's too draining for her."

"Oh gods." I rubbed my hand across my face. "Is he okay?"

"The longer he gets to rest between now and the next Trial, the better. I, erm…" She looked at me guiltily. "I sedated him."

"You sedated him?"

"It was the only way I could get him to rest. He has to let his body regenerate, or the stone will take over," she said apologetically. "If we can keep him unconscious for a full day, and he barely uses any power when he wakes, then he stands a chance of surviving another Trial." She squeezed my shoulders as she spoke, trying to reassure me. She was only partially successful.

I needed to know about Atlantis. I needed to know if

the Font of Zoi was an alternative to an even more awful decision.

*Poseidon, or Lily.*

If it were just those two, then the choice would be my sister. But it wasn't that simple.

Tears filled my eyes, unbidden.

Persephone pulled me into to her, wrapping her arms around me. "Hey, it's okay, we'll save him," she said. "You'll save him."

That only made the tears fall faster. "But saving him… Saving him means…" I tried to get the words out, but my throat closed again, the numbness that had fallen over me in my solitude abandoning me.

Persephone held me at arm's length, looking into my face and frowning with concern. "Saving him means what?" Realization washed over her features. "The Oracle didn't give you good news, did she?"

I shook my head, and she moved past me, into my room to pick up Kryvo's cushion. "Take your clever little friend, and we'll go to my place. You need fixing up, and if you tell me whatever that mountain-top dwelling weirdo said to you, we'll work it out together."

"Wow," squeaked Kryvo, as we materialized in what I assumed was Persephone's place.

It was as though a greenhouse had had a baby with a gothic castle. The whole structure was made from intricate wrought iron, and almost every wall between the iron frame was made from glass. Gold and red roses were intertwined around the iron, a stark contrast to the mass of green beyond the glass walls. It looked like a luscious jungle out there, with hundreds of types of trees and plants growing beside each other. Even someone as lacking in plant knowledge as I could see that a lot of the species shouldn't be found growing side by side.

"Wow," I repeated the starfish's word. I refocused on the room we were in, seeing that it was a large living and dining room in one. The floor was a rich dark wood, and the dining area was raised a few steps to separate it. An iron chandelier hung low over an organic-shaped tabletop made from one beautiful slab of polished wood. In front of the glass walls, surrounding a fire dish flickering with a warm glow, were a series of huge chintzy pink armchairs. Green potted ferns dotted the room, and there were brightly colored orchids on many of the surfaces.

I tipped my head back to look up, seeing the lofty ceiling far above us, glittering with lights that looked like stars.

"You like it?" Persephone smiled at me.

"It's stunning."

"We can only live here six months of the year. On the surface of the underworld, I mean. The rest of the time we have to live underground, in Hades' palace. I had a lot of windows to make up for when I designed this place."

"I'd love to hear how you two got together," I said, as she led me to the armchairs.

"And I'd love to tell you, but not now. We've got some more important matters to attend to. Sit."

I did, and she moved to a long counter along the back of the dining area. She clattered around a few moments, and I let the comfy couch take my weight, closing my eyes and trying to clear and organize my thoughts so that I could make some sort of sense to my new friend.

"So. Tell me what happened with the Oracle."

I opened my eyes, and she was pulling leaves off a couple of plants and putting them into a small mortar. She ground them up, and vines snaked from her palms, wrapping around the stone bowl.

I watched with fascination. "What are you doing?"

"Making something that will restore your strength faster than those vials Poseidon has been giving you."

"Thank you."

"You're welcome. Now, tell me."


As calmly as I could, I told Persephone what the Oracle had said. I tried to keep my emotion at bay, delivering the information as concisely as possible. By the time I had told her everything though, silent tears were streaming down my cheeks again.

She walked over to me, handing me a steaming mug of something that smelled like blackcurrants. I took it, and sipped cautiously. Warmth spread through my whole body.

"I'm so sorry, Almi. This is a seriously shitty situation to be in." Persephone's face was filled with sympathy as she sat down on the armchair next to mine.

"Lily says we are destined to save the world together. She says she's not mad or upset about it."

Persephone's face creased into a frown, concern

replacing the sympathy. "Lily says?" she repeated. "I thought she's been unconscious for years?"

I let out a long breath as I realized what I'd said. I hadn't meant to tell her that I spoke to Lily. The words had slipped out, my control over myself and my emotions was so tenuous. "I talk to her in my head," I admitted quietly. "I get a really vivid image of her, and she talks back."

Persephone looked surprised, then thoughtful. "Do you think it's actually her?"

I shrugged. "At first, I thought it was my grief and loneliness, when I was in the human world with nobody to turn to. But...she's so much like her, not me. She thinks of things I don't, and she knows things I don't. Which makes me wonder if I even could be making her up myself."

"You would be amazed what our subconscious knows about us that we don't," said Persephone gently.

"So you think I'm making her up?"

"I don't know. You said she had powerful magic when she was awake?"

"Yes."

"Any telepathic magic?"

"Erm, no. Just water."

"Hmm. Well, either way, she told you she is not upset about you embracing your power to find the Heart of the Ocean?"

I swallowed hard. "She was always selfless. But I've spent my whole adult life trying to save her. I can't give up now. I can't." Desperation perforated my every word.

I expected Persephone to tell me that the right thing to

33

do was let Lily die in order to save everyone else. I knew that was what any sane person would tell me to do. But she didn't.

"What about Atlantis?" she asked.

"The Oracle told Poseidon he had to tell me something about it."

"Something that would help cure the blight?"

I bit my lip as I remembered what the deity had said. "She said there was no way to cure the blight without the Heart of the Ocean. And the only way to get it was for me to get my full power." My shoulders sagged.

"There has to be a way around this."

I looked at her determined expression. "You think?"

"Yes. Prophecies are almost as tricky as gods. There's always another way."

A surge of hope flooded my system as I gripped the mug. All I'd needed was to hear someone else say there might be another way. "Do you have any ideas?"

"No. You have to survive the Trials and keep Poseidon alive. And I don't see how you can do that without your magic."

I sat back guiltily. "I think I may have pissed my air magic off. In the temple."

Persephone looked alarmed. "How?"

"I kind of said I didn't want it."

"Right. Well. Hopefully, there was no harm done and you can just apologize?"

"Apollo said air was fickle, and hard to control."

"Hmm. We'll work on that next. In the meantime, what are you going to do about the love thing?"

"Love thing?"

She looked at me like I'd just suffered a head injury. "Almi, if you fall in love with your husband, you're going to die. Does that not strike you as something we need to address?"

I held my hand up. "Whoa, now. There is a whole load of reasons why that does not cause me concern right now." I drained the contents of my mug, already feeling stronger. "Number one, he's a massive grumpy idiot who represents everything I can't stand in life. Number two, I wouldn't even know how to fall in love. I love my sister, and that's it. I have no capacity or desire to love anyone else. Number three, I'll only die if the love is reciprocated." I looked pointedly at Persephone. "So, nothing to worry about."

She just stared at me, eyes wide and brows raised.

"What?" I said, unable to take the long silence.

"I'm trying to work out where to even begin," she said.

"You mentioned wine?"

Persephone nodded. "Wine is a very good place to begin."

# ALMI

When we both had glasses of something amber-colored and fizzy, Persephone cleared her throat. "I think you're in more danger than you think, Almi."

"In what way?"

"I'm not going to risk moving you closer to that danger, but you need to be more prepared than you currently are."

"I'm not following you."

"I am not going to say anything to make you like Poseidon any more than you do now."

"In case you accidentally make me fall in love with him?" I scoffed.

She didn't laugh. In fact, she looked as serious as I'd ever seen her. "Almi, I'd bet my entire life and everything I own on one thing. He loves you."

I scowled. "Lily thinks so too. But you guys don't know what the marriage bond is like." I paused. "Well, maybe you do, since you're married to his brother. This constant pull toward each other, this weird electricity thing we get whenever we touch - it could so easily be misinterpreted as something more."

Persephone's green eyes filled with something that could have been sorrow. "Almi, if it turns into something more, you'll die. You get that, right?"

"Yes, but I don't love him. And I don't think he loves me. He might be drawn to me, and fancy me, but that's not love."

"What happened at Aphrodite's palace?"

My cheeks heated. "We, erm, you know…"

"You had sex?" She looked almost relieved.

"No. But we were, erm, close." I swallowed, and decided to bare heart and soul. After all, there wasn't much she didn't know about me anymore. "I haven't been with anyone before, and he stopped it before it went any further because of that."

"Oh gods." Persephone rubbed her hand over her pale face. "Almi, no guy, god, or anything with a damn dick, is going to turn down sex unless love is involved!"

"Oh," I said, my cheeks burning now. I took a long glug of wine. "Oh," I said again, at a loss for any other words to say.

Could the fierce sea god really love me?

How? He barely even knew me. Surely he couldn't fall in love with someone within a week?

"Poseidon has been sullen and angry since I've known him. But that wild look in his eyes when he looks at you? I have never seen that before. And the anger is different now. Not humming under the surface, but clawing to get free. He is different around you, for sure."

"Oh." In an attempt to use another word than *oh*, I looked down at Kryvo, who was stuck to my collarbone. "What do you think, Kryvo?" I prayed the starfish would say the sea god thought I was odd and wanted nothing to with me.

No sooner than I had the thought was it followed by a prickle of alarm.

*I didn't want Poseidon to want nothing to do with me.*

Shit. Flashes of the way he had made me feel in Aphrodite's palace came to me, and I buried them quickly.

"You keep kissing him when I'm stuck to you," the starfish said, matter-of-factly.

"That's not an opinion."

"You two are connected. There is an energy between you, and the magic you both have binds."

I thought about our ride on Blue and Chrysos, and the way our power had merged in the last Trial. More unease washed through me.

"We are connected," I repeated. "Not in love. There's a difference."

"You need to be careful. Try not to spend too much time alone with him," said Persephone.

"How? We have to finish the Trials. Or at least, *try* to finish the Trials." I drank more wine. "This is a fucking mess," I muttered.

Persephone gave me a sympathetic look that turned quickly to resolute. "Concentrate on surviving the Trials, hold on to the things about Poseidon that piss you off, and then we'll work out the Heart of the Ocean. That's the plan."

"Yes." It wasn't a new plan, but it was the only one we had. And I wasn't doing it alone. I knew the woman beside me would help me, no matter what. I reached out and squeezed her hand, a movement uncharacteristic for me, but it felt right. "Thank you. Lily has been my only friend for a long time. I'm so grateful for your help."

She squeezed my hand back. "I could do with a friend here, too, and I think you're great."

Warmth flowed through me again, along with hope.

We would find another way.

We talked for another hour or so, and Persephone seemed to make a point of picking subjects that had nothing to do with the Trials or Lily or Poseidon. We talked about the human world, about where she grew up in New York and the life I'd lived in my trailer. We talked about music and movies and the sorts of things normal people got to talk about.

When Hades flashed into the room, I nearly dropped my drink in surprise.

"Oh, I didn't know you had company," he said, moving to Persephone and bending down to kiss her. "How is Poseidon?"

"He needs to sleep. And Almi had an unsettling visit with the Oracle." Hades looked at me, understanding swirling in his silver eyes. "That woman could be described as a lot worse than unsettling." He eyed the wine in my hand. "Be careful," he told me. "Persephone has a volatile history with Dionysus' wine."

I raised an eyebrow, and she giggled. "When I was human, I couldn't handle it. You're not human, you'll be fine," she reassured me.

A flash drew all our attentions to the flame dish. Flames roared up high, bright white, then fell away to reveal an image of Atlas' face. A long silver scratch ran down the side of his face, and I gasped in surprise. Had that happened during the fight I was spirited away from?

"Good evening, Olympus." His voice was hard and dry, all his charm gone. "The next Trial will be the last of the Poseidon Trials."

Relief hammered through me. I glanced at Persephone and saw the same feeling mirrored on her face. "Thank the gods for that."

"It is time the world knew what the King of the Ocean is capable of. What kind of a god he truly is." My skin tightened, and I leaned forward. "I was the ruler of a great city in Olympus once. My wife and I ruled happily, until Poseidon interfered." Red flames burst to life in his irises and then began to lick over his skin.

"Fuck," Hades swore.

"The god you all revere sank my city to the bottom of the ocean. He was responsible for the deaths of hundreds of innocent people."

The sound of blood pounding in my ears got louder. "No," I whispered.

"And I only wish that the fate that befell my beloved wife was as simple as death," the Titan snarled. "For the final

Trial, our competitors will navigate my sunken city, and find as many shells as they can. But be warned; the monsters there are worse than anything in the shallows. Time in the depths has turned my once great city into a lethal maze, and rotbloods will be the least of your worries. You begin at dawn. Find my city, find the shells. End the Trials."

The flames flashed up again, swallowing the image. When they died down, Atlas was gone.

"Shit," Hades swore again. The temperature in the room increased. I stared numbly at the fire.

"Did he really kill hundreds of people and sink an entire city?" My words were a mumble.

"You must ask him," Hades' said. "It is not my place to speak of it."

"War can be brutal," said Persephone gently.

"This was before the war," Hades muttered. "These two have had a rivalry going back centuries, but my brother would never tell me what happened."

"He said he was ashamed," I said quietly.

Hades looked at me. "He told you of it?"

"No. He told me he didn't want to speak of it because he was ashamed."

Hades let out a long sigh. "We have all done things of which we are ashamed. None more so than the gods."

"You've killed hundreds of innocent people?" I snapped, then regretted it when I saw his grave face.

"I am the God of Death," he said, power ringing out around him. "I have done things you can't even begin to imagine."

Persephone got up slowly from her chair, the move-

41

ment diffusing the power rolling from Hades. "I will have to wake him earlier than I'd hoped," she said gently.

Hades looked at her, then nodded. "He needs to tell his wife what he has done. They need to make a plan to get through this."

# ALMI

*P*ersephone flashed us back to the palace, directly to Poseidon's throne room. I looked at the giant wave throne, the surly god distinctly absent.

"I'll bring him here when I've woken him," Persephone said, then flashed away.

I let out a long breath, then heard a cough behind me. Whirling, I saw Galatea. She had a huge bruise under her left eye, and her staff was scratched.

"Galatea, what happened?"

"I was going to ask you the same." She looked tired, but her blue eyes were alert as always. She leaned against a statue of an orca and glanced at the huge throne. "He flashed me out of there."

"Me too." He had removed both of his allies. Two women who had power and could have helped him. "Fucking idiot." I shook my head.

Galatea flinched, but she didn't reprimand me for blaspheming. "My sentiments also," she said. "I understand the dragon and Persephone have healed him."

"Yes. Persephone says he won't be able to use much power when he comes round."

Galatea nodded. "You saw Atlas' announcement about the last Trial?" Her words were tentative, and I nodded. "And the part about him sinking a city?" I nodded again. She took a long breath. "I do not know the full story, but trust me when I tell you that Poseidon is not a cruel god. He never has been."

"Is he... a murderer?"

"There are no gods in Olympus not responsible for death," she said resignedly. "But Poseidon has a good heart."

She would say that, though, she was unwaveringly loyal to the sea god.

"Well, I hope he will tell me about both Atlas, and Atlantis, when he is roused," I said. Even as the words left my mouth, something in my mind clicked.

Galatea looked intently at me. "They are one and the same, Almi."

My mind whirred as I stared back at her.

*Atlas.*

*Atlantis.*

"Atlantis is Atlas' city?"

Galatea nodded. "Yes. It was named for him. It was a magnificent city, with enough power to rival a realm."

"And a font that could create life," I murmured.

Galatea frowned. "How do you know of that?"

"She knows more than she thinks she does." Poseidon's voice rang out behind us, and we both turned.

He was standing tall, wearing the tight blue pants and no shirt, straps holding weapons criss-crossing his chest.

But half his chest was the color of granite. It snaked up his neck, just creeping over the left side of his jaw.

My heart seemed to slow in my chest as I looked at him, his wild eyes boring into mine.

"What happened between you and Atlas?" demanded Galatea before I could say a word. I couldn't help admiring the authority in her tone as she addressed her king. This woman was not taking no for an answer, no matter who she was speaking to.

"We had a conversation." Poseidon's voice was laced with barely restrained anger, but I didn't think it was directed at her. Galatea banged her staff on the ground, not bothering to try to restrain her own anger.

"Sire, you could have been killed! What were you thinking, sending both me and Almi away? We do not need protecting, you do!"

"Yeah!" Galatea's outburst had summed up my feelings exactly.

Poseidon turned his angry eyes to his general. "Do you really believe, for even a moment, that I think you incapable or weak?" Galatea said nothing, but doubt flickered through her eyes. "I removed both of you because I knew what was coming, and it was not something either of you could help with."

"We're back to this cryptic bullshit again?" I fisted my hands on my hips, my patience at its end. Persephone had fixed my body with her tea, but emotionally I was spent. "I'm done only getting half the story, Poseidon. You hear me? Done." I folded my arms over my chest and glared at him.

He looked between me and Galatea, then let out a long

breath. "Atlas' wife is not a foe either of you can face."

"Why not? I threw a water Titan half a damned mile through the ocean, and Galatea is as hard as nails!"

"I will tell you what happened, but you must let me start at the start."

I dropped my arms. "Fine."

"We shall go the east wing."

"Why?"

"There is a painting. It will help me to make you understand."

Make me understand? That did not sound good. Trepidation coursed through me as I turned to follow him out of the throne room.

Galatea coughed again, and he turned. "Sire... I apologize for my outburst. If this is a conversation you wish to have with your wife alone, then I trust you to keep me informed later."

Poseidon gave her a tiny, grateful smile. Not the full-on smile that had seared itself into my brain, but a rare expression, nonetheless. "I will appraise you of what we are facing as soon as we are back from the east wing. Thank you, Galatea."


We didn't exchange a single word as we walked through the halls of the palace. The further we got, the more nervous I became. How the hell had I not made the connection between Atlas and Atlantis before? The Titan had named the city after himself, and I'd totally failed to notice the names were connected.

Would it have made any difference if I had realized?

Probably not. But it explained why Poseidon had been so reluctant to talk about the sunken city. I tried to recall what the book had said about it. Clearly the author had been lacking some vital information.

I wrung my hands as we made our way down a long winding staircase, natural light diminishing, and the glass walls replaced by white marble.

I felt like a leaf bobbing along a river, or a feather floating on the breeze—all my grounding gone, and nowhere to cling to for comfort.

My time with Persephone had helped re-instate my hope for Lily. Rather, it had made me believe that there could be — *had to be* — another way to save everyone without losing her.

But when it came to Poseidon...I didn't know how to feel. I didn't understand anything about being a god. Not only a god, one of the three most powerful, ruling gods of Olympus. The power and responsibility he wielded, the friendships and threats he would have faced in his life.... His life was worlds away from mine. Galatea had just referred to me as his wife, but that wasn't how it felt, despite the undeniable bond between us.

As if hearing my thoughts, he glanced over his shoulder at me. His white hair was swept back with a simple gold circlet, and I had a clear view of his stormy eyes.

Could I trust him? Had he been the cause of hundreds of innocents' deaths, as Atlas had said? What if he was about to show me how horrific he really was?

What if the reason he was so damn miserable was because he was truly bad at his core.

*What if I was bound to a monster?*

# ALMI

*W*e entered a room at the bottom of a dark staircase. It was gloomy, and the air was musty, a slightly damp scent to it. Drapes hung along the walls, and they were covered in thick dust. The only light came from the ceiling, which glowed, just like the one in my room but more faintly. Poseidon clapped his hands quietly, and the light increased enough that I could see properly.

The room was much longer than I originally thought, and lining both sides were statues. Some marble, some stone, and many broken. A dark blue carpet ran down the middle, and when I stepped onto it a cloud of dust rose around my feet.

"There are no starfish in here," Kryvo squeaked, so only I could hear him.

So Kryvo hadn't seen anything in this room before. I peered at the first statue as we started down the carpet. It was of a satyr, holding up a set of panpipes and looking devilishly cheerful. A flash of concern filled me that these were people who been afflicted by the stone blight, but that thought fled when I reached out and touched it. It looked nothing like the stone that had been creeping over Lily's limbs or crawling across Poseidon's face. That stone was dark grey and mottled. This was ash-veined white marble. And the satyr looked happy, not like a being about to be turned to stone.

We kept walking, and I noticed that very few of the statues were of sea creatures — unlike the rest of the palace. Maybe that's why Kryvo's starfish friends were absent.

When we were halfway down the hall, Poseidon stopped. Reaching out, he gripped the edge of a set of dusty red drapes, and tugged hard. The fabric fell to the floor, the metal pole coming with it and clattering on the tiles as a huge cloud of dust puffed up around us.

When it cleared, I saw the mural painted on the wall behind the drapes.

I took a step back before I'd realized my legs had moved. Kryvo heated on my collarbone, as goosebumps rose across my skin.

The green hand.

I was looking at what that green hand had been attached to.

And I'd seen the creature before, but not like this... It was the same as statue in the last trial that we had found hidden behind the lavafall. A beautiful woman with snakes for hair.

But here... Here she was portrayed very differently.

Her figure was lunging out of the painting, so lifelike it had startled me. The snakes covering her head were all standing on end, teeth bared, evil in their eyes and their scales gleaming gold. Her whole body was green and scaled, her long taloned hands scratching at the viewer of the image. And her eyes... They were reptilian—bright yellow and slitted vertically.

The haunting beauty of the woman was still there, under the ferocious anger. Humanity resided in those snake-like eyes, I was sure. Her high, dignified cheek-bones, and beautiful, full red lips spoke of what she had once been.

I knew with utter certainty who I was looking at.

"Atlas' wife."

"Yes. She was not in this form when he married her."

I turned to Poseidon, my breath a little short. "What happened to her?" I dropped my voice, almost not wanting to know the answer. "Did you do this to her?"

Poseidon's eyes burned bright blue a moment, and I expected him to drop my gaze. But he held it. "No."

Relief flooded me.

"But I am responsible."

My stomach tightened again. "How?"

"Her name is Medusa. Atlas and I were close once, and I was very fond of Medusa, until I unwittingly discovered that she had a human lover. That is not uncommon amongst the gods, and I agreed to say nothing when she told me there was no seriousness to the affair. But the man she was betraying her husband with died. She came to me, knowing that I was powerful and had the ear of Zeus and Hades. She begged me to bring her lover back. I refused. Bringing life back from the dead is a power only all twelve Olympians can achieve, and they must all agree. Doing so would have been akin to me taking a stand against Atlas. Using the Olympians to save the lover of my friend's wife was not something I was willing to do." He let out a long sigh and looked back at the painting. "I underestimated her grief and determination. Atlas is a primordial Titan, and his city housed one of the most powerful artifacts ever created. Not even the gods know how it was created."

"The Font of Zoi," I breathed.

"Yes. While Atlas was visiting with Zeus, Medusa stole into the palace and tried to use the Font to bring back her lover. The Font turned on her. It created life, but in the form of a monster. And it used her body as a vessel."

I shuddered as I looked from his face back to the painting. "I read the font only backfired if used will ill-intent," I whispered.

"She was grief-stricken, and angry. With me. The massive surge of power from the font reached me first, because Atlantis was so close to my realm. I got to the palace before anyone else did. She was turning before my eyes, and I could do nothing to stop it happening. Through her pain, she told me that me and my realm would pay. I believe she had tried to use the font not just to bring back her lover, but to inflict harm on me or Aquarius. When Atlas and Zeus arrived moments later, she rose as you see her here. She told Atlas I had tried to seduce her, then used the Font to turn her into a monster when she had refused. If my brother, Zeus, hadn't been there, Atlas would have killed me on the spot. Hades arrived, and we fought, only defeating Atlas as more Olympians arrived to help. We combined our powers to banish Atlas. It is not possible to kill a Titan, but we were able to send him into an indefinite sleep."

He looked back at me, his eyes bright and intense. "Medusa escaped though. And she has the power to turn people to stone."

"Stone," I repeated. A sick feeling rolled through my gut as the pieces snapped into place.

"Stone. Before I could catch her, she had turned the entire population of Atlantis to stone. If you look into her eyes, you become a statue."

"Did you look into her eyes?"

"Yes, but I am a god. I was not affected. At the time."

"What did you do with her?"

He took a breath. "I didn't know if there was any chance of saving the people in Atlantis. But the Font was too dangerous to be used again, and I knew Medusa was too dangerous to be allowed to live."

"So you sank Atlantis."

He nodded. "Yes. And I bound her to the city."

"She sank with it?"

"Yes."

"She's spent centuries trapped alone in a city full of statues she created at the bottom of the ocean?" The horror of it made me feel even more sick.

"It was that or kill her."

I honestly wasn't sure which was worse. "And when Zeus woke up Atlas, he went down to Atlantis, found her and freed her?"

"Yes. I believe the golden snakes Galatea has been

tracking are spreading the blight, and I think Atlas created them in Medusa's honor. And to make it clear to me that I deserve this. This is Atlas' revenge. He wants to turn my realm to stone, as he believes I made his own wife do to his."

"And that means… As your wife, he wants to turn me into a monster?"

Light flared in Poseidon's eyes, waves crashing over his irises. "The last Trial is in Atlantis. The Font is in Atlantis." He nodded gravely. "I do believe that is what he will try to do."

# ALMI

*I* stared at Poseidon, my mind reeling.

Part of me was relieved. Relieved that the god before me wasn't the brute I had feared he was. Relieved that my gut was right, that the connection I had with him had read his soul, and his heart, correctly.

And at least so much of what was happening to Aquarius and its king made sense to me now. I had no idea how Lily and her sleeping sickness fit into anything, and I still knew nothing about the Heart of the Ocean, but Atlas and the stone blight... "It's a perfect revenge," I said softly, looking back at the image of Medusa.

"Yes. I do not know if I was infected by Medusa's stare centuries ago, and it only flared up when he freed her, or if I have been infected like everyone else has. Galatea believes the snakes are passing the blight to the citizens."

"And you think Atlas created the snakes? They are not a part of Medusa's magic?"

"No, I think he created them so that I would know what they meant."

I looked back at him. "Did you not suspect Atlas when people started turning to stone?"

"Nobody has seen the Titans for centuries. The ones we managed to send to sleep vanished from their prisons as one, many years ago and we still do not know who was responsible. Until Oceanus was found and awoken last year, the original, primordial Titans were presumed lost to the world."

I blinked at him, reminded once more of how different his life must have been from mine. "Do you think he could use the font to turn me into..." I pointed at the painting. "That?"

Distant thunder rolled, and a tendril of stone wound across his cheek. "I will not allow him to."

"You mustn't use any power," I said, instinctively reaching out and touching his arm. A protective surge made me want to close the gap and embrace him, but something stopped me.

Sensing my hesitation, he spoke again. "I did not want to remove you and Galatea from the bakery. But I do not know a way of defending against the stone stare of the snakes, other than by being a god. I had no choice." His words were earnest and soft, and any residual anger I had melted away.

"Honestly, looking at her, I'm sort of glad you did," I whispered back. "Why do you even have this painting in here?"

"It is impossible for most to look at her directly, so I kept a painting, in case I ever needed to show a mortal."

"Why, if you thought you'd sent her to the bottom of the ocean for eternity?" I suppressed another shudder.

Emotion filled his eyes and they moved to her reptilian ones in the picture. "I could have asked the Olympians to bring him back. Her lover. And I didn't. She went mad with grief."

"Are you sure she wasn't nuts to begin with?"

"She was vibrant, and clever, and perhaps a little cruel." He tilted his head, lost in his memory. "But the pain of grief is real."

I nodded. "Yes." The thought of losing my sister was unbearable. And now, the thought of losing Poseidon, Kryvo, or Persephone sent stabs of fear and denial through me too.

"I didn't know how deeply she loved him."

"Would it have changed your decision to help her if you had?"

He didn't answer for a while. Then he turned his head, fixing his eyes on me. "Many things have changed since then," he said quietly.

"Is that a yes?"

His hair fell forward across his face as he shook his head. "No." He lifted an arm, gesturing at the image. "I suppose I painted this to remind me that she had once been human. And that decisions have consequences. Even the decisions of a god and a king."

The magnitude of his words sunk in slowly, and for the first time, I had a clear picture of the man standing in front of me.

He understood love and grief. He felt regret, remorse, and responsibility. He didn't take his position as a god and a king lightly, even a fraction. His rigid control and his seriousness all suddenly made sense.

He feared making the wrong decision.

He feared losing control, because he understood, and feared, the consequences of his actions so keenly.

There could be no impulse decisions, no spontaneous actions — because he wouldn't know or be able to control the outcome.

Everything had to be measured, weighed, and evaluated, lest the consequences be as dire as Medusa.

I stared up at him, trying to work out what to say. I felt like I'd been given a window into the man's soul, a glimpse of the god that I shouldn't have. And it unsettled me a little. Not because I feared him, but the opposite. My respect for him was growing by the second. And for someone like me, respect was everything.

I pulled at the least serious thing I could, unwilling to go any deeper into his mind.

"You painted this? You're pretty good."

"I paint better seascapes," he said, and I could hear a quirk of dry amusement in his low voice.

I stepped into him, winding my arms around his waist, and pressing my face to his solid chest. He tensed a moment, then his hand traced its way down my spine, before flattening on the small of my back and pulling me harder into his body.

I wanted to kiss him, so badly. I wanted him to know I understood, and that he had done nothing wrong. That Medusa would probably have flipped out and fucked everything up on her own. But I dared not say a thing that would risk deepening our bond. *Risk making my heart ache for him any more than it was starting to.*

"We must work out a way to survive, and win, the

Atlantis Trial," said Poseidon, and I was relieved that he was changing the subject to something more practical.

And he was right. I needed to find a way to get air to work with me enough to survive the damn Trial and keep Poseidon alive, but not enough to fully embrace my power and kill my sister.

"I think I pissed off my air magic," I said into his chest.

"Then you'd better apologize."

## ALMI

*a* weirdly comfortable silence fell between us as he led me out of the dusty hall and back up the winding staircases of the palace.

"You know, we could get to the pegasus stables a lot quicker if you let me flash us there," Poseidon said, giving me a sideways glance. I'd told him not to flash us anywhere, as despite his protests that it didn't use much magic, I figured the fact that only gods could do it suggested otherwise.

"I want to see how to get there without flashing," I said. Which was partially true. I was nervous about trying to talk to air again. The platform at the top of the stables was the perfect place to try though, given that it was the place I'd first connected consciously with my magic. Plus, I would get to see Blue.

"You can't," Poseidon said.

"What?"

"You can't reach my personal stables without flashing."

"Then how are we going to get there?"

He threw me another glance, and I swore I could see a hint of excitement in the look. "The palace has secrets."

"Tell me about it," I said.

He quirked an eyebrow. "You have seen some of them?"

I looked briefly down at the starfish attached to my skin. "Yep."

He followed my look, and his brows drew together. I thought he would ask more, but he said nothing.

I followed him all the way to his throne room, where he moved to a towering statue of a merman. It was at the back of the round room, and the figure had his head tilted back and a trident pointed at the ceiling. The marble merman was as tall as Poseidon, which he demonstrated by reaching up and gripping the middle prong of the trident, which few would have been able to reach.

Blue light rippled across the room, and a loud click sounded. I gasped as the ceiling above us began to change, bright light flooding through the intricate images painted there.

Within moments, the domed ceiling had vanished completely, and clear sky showed above us, the pastel-colored clouds of Olympus rolling over us.

"But… but… we're underwater?"

Poseidon's lips quirked, then he put his fingers to his lips and whistled. Nothing happened for a moment, then two tiny dots appeared in the bright sky above us. Blue and Chrysos came into focus as they flew down toward us, and my heart filled with happiness to see the pegasus.

"Blue!" He landed gracefully in front of me, looking

massive and regal in the throne room. I reached out, running my hand along his snout. He snorted happily.

"Ready?" Poseidon had moved next to me, and he gripped my waist when I nodded, lifting me easily onto the pegasus. Blue stamped his feet, and we took off.

As soon as the fresh ocean air hit me, I felt a trickle of calm penetrate the emotional churn of the last few hours. I closed my eyes, gripping Blue's mane and letting the breeze engulf me.

"I'm sorry if I gave you the impression that I didn't want you," I said out loud. My words were a whisper, the wind snatching them from my lips as I spoke them. "The thing is, I love my sister. And embracing you might kill her." I took a deep breath as I felt Blue swoop and a big gust of air blew over me, making my hair whip around my face. "And that would... Well, it would break me. Into a million pieces. That could never be put back together again." I thought I felt the wind still for a fraction of a second, before it gusted around me even harder. "Do you think we can do what we were doing before? You help me out, just until I work all of this out?"

I opened one eye hopefully, then the other.

A little whirlwind whipped around me, lifting Blue's mane and bouncing off my arms.

"Hello!" I said gleefully. The sight of my little air friend filled me with as much joy as seeing Blue did, and not because I needed the magic. Because I *wanted* it.

The whirlwind zoomed away, and I twisted to watch it make for Poseidon and Chrysos. With a flourish, it spun around the sea god, lifting his hair, then Chrysos' tail. The gold pegasus whinnied and kicked out in annoyance, and I laughed aloud.

Chrysos sped up so that Poseidon was right alongside me. "It looks like you've been forgiven," the god said drily, eyeing the mischievous little tornado as it whooshed after him.

I beamed at him. "It looks that way."

My smile seemed to soften him, and a faint shadow of my grin tugged at his lips. "We must go to my ship. I would like to show you around before we set out on this last Trial." There was a grave finality to his words that I didn't like at all.

"Can I get my stuff first?"

"Yes. I need to appraise Galatea of what we are facing in Medusa. I should have told her before now."

"Probably."

"Take Blue back to the throne room and pack your things. I will meet you on the ship in an hour."

# ALMI

I stared down at the belt on my bed, everything I owned rammed into the bewitched pockets.

"I think that's everything," I said.

"Why are you speaking like you're not coming back?" Kryvo's nerves were evident in his squeaky voice.

"I'm not sure," I lied.

There had been an undeniable finality in Poseidon's tone when he'd told me to come and pack, and I knew he felt the same way I did.

This was it. The last Trial.

If any of Atlas' cronies won, it was game over. If I accidentally embraced my full power and killed my sister, I didn't know what I would do, but I was pretty sure it wouldn't involve coming back to the palace. And if I felt any more strongly about the complicated, tortured god who held the title of my husband... Well, that might be game over, too. That was, if Persephone was right, and he loved me.

Shaking off the thought, I picked up the belt and

strapped it on. For the first time, I felt appropriately dressed for a Trial. I felt strong and alert, probably thanks to Persephone's healing magic. The shell tattoo was three-quarters filled with color, but my desire to admire it had vanished.

"Are you sure you want to come with me?" I asked Kryvo.

"I'm not going to dignify that with an answer," he said huffily.

I smiled. "Just checking. I knew you wouldn't abandon me at the last hurdle," I told him. He heated on my skin.

"Can we take my cushion please? I think it may be a long trip to the bottom of the ocean."

I picked up his cushion and stowed it in the belt.

It probably would be a long trip. And if the author of the book had got anything right, it was a dangerous one, too. Poseidon no longer had any control over the creatures that inhabited the sea's depths.

I sucked in a breath. "So. My goals are," I raised my hand and ticked them off on my fingers. "Reach Atlantis without being eaten, find the most shells and win the Trial, use my power without fully embracing it, don't fall in love, and don't get turned into a monster by a primordial, all powerful god."

"You forgot cure the stone blight and save Aquarius."

"Shit."

"Shit," repeated the little starfish.

~

65

When I got back to the throne room, I was surprised to see not only Poseidon there, but Hades, Persephone, and Galatea.

"I made you these," said Persephone, stepping forward and handing me four vials of brown liquid. "It's the tea from my place, but I've added a little extra. It will heal most mild-to-serious wounds, but only with rest."

"Thank you," I said gratefully, tucking them into a pouch on my belt.

"I hope you don't need them. And I'm sorry we can't help you more," she said, before wrapping me in a warm hug. "Know that we would if we could."

"I know," I told her. She stepped back, and Hades' stare caught my eye.

*Look after my brother,* he said, but his voice sounded in my mind. I nodded. Galatea stepped forward, holding her hand out formally.

"I want you to know that I believe you to be the best chance our king has. And that I am confident that you will save our realm from destruction." I took her proffered hand, trying to suppress an awkward grin as she shook it.

"I'll do my best," I said.

"I know you will. By the way, I still think you're odd." She gave me a true smile, her face lighting up with wry amusement.

Impulsively, I tugged on her arm, pulling her into a brief hug. She stiffened and looked a little alarmed when I pushed her away again.

"I've decided to own being odd."

"Probably for the best," she nodded. "Look, I want you to have something." She pulled her dagger from its sheath and handed it to me. It was the one she had lent me for the last Trial.

"But…" She had given me the strong impression that the dagger was important to her before, and the intricate carving on the handle suggested it was valuable. I looked up from the dagger to her. "This is yours."

"And now it is yours. If I can't be involved in taking down that scumbag Atlas, then at least you can take my weapon into battle with you."

"Are you sure?"

"I am. You have earned it, Almi."

"Thank you. I am honored."

"Prove it, by winning."

I nodded and tucked the knife into the strap on my leg —now on the outside of my tight leather pants.

"Are you ready?" Poseidon asked.

I looked around the throne room. All the people here had become my friends, including Kryvo and Blue. I felt a surge of reluctance to leave, the idea of there not being a bunch of life-threatening shit going on around us and being able to just enjoy time with these people, suddenly filling my mind.

I'd never wanted anything other than Lily before. And now…? Now I wanted a life. In this place, with these people.

I still wanted Lily. Jeez, did I still want Lily. But I wanted Lily to meet my new friends, enjoy their company, play with my air magic, explore the Palace, feel what it was like to ride Blue — and a hundred other things this life could offer us.

"Almi?" Poseidon's voice was soft and broke me from my unexpected reverie.

"Yes. I'm sorry. I'm ready." I looked at Persephone. "Thanks for everything. If we don't see each other again, you saved my life, and, as soppy as it sounds, proved to me that I can have friends." I looked at Galatea. "You too. Thank you both."

Persephone gave me an encouraging smile, and Galatea looked even more awkward. "We'll see you just as soon as you're back," Persephone said firmly.

"Preferably victorious and with his trident returned," added Hades, nodding at his brother.

Poseidon gave him a look, then lifted me onto Blue's back. I closed my eyes quickly, allowing just a second for the emotion to wash over me. Then, gathering my resolve, I squeezed the pegasus with my thighs. "Let's go, Blue," I whispered, and the pegasus launched himself into the air.

As soon as we reached the empty sky above Aquarius, my little whirlwind appeared, dancing around us as we soared higher.

I couldn't see Poseidon's ship anywhere, but Blue seemed to know where he was going, so I clung on and enjoyed the ride.

After a few moments, we burst through a large, coral-colored cloud, and as if a veil was lifted, Poseidon's gleaming ship was revealed in all its magnificence. Blue touched down on the bridge and Poseidon landed a few feet away. His hair was windswept, and his emotionally charged gaze fell on me as he leaped down from Chrysos.

"You care for them." It was a statement, not a question.

He strode toward me with an almost alarming sense of purpose. I eased myself down from Blue's back.

"Yes."

"You earned the respect of my general and my brother."

"More by luck than by judgement, I think," I shrugged awkwardly. Poseidon came to a stop a foot away from me.

"You are more than you think you are, Almi." Storm clouds swept across his eyes.

"Perhaps." A few days ago, I would have argued. But with my unfolding power, and the responsibility of so many lives weighing on me, I *had* to be more than I thought I was. I didn't have a choice.

"I wish I could show you."

I frowned at his words. "Show me what?"

He shook his head. Tight control gradually retook his features, the storm in his eyes dying away. "The ship. I need to show you the ship."

Normally, I would have pushed him to find out what he had really been about to say. But in my gut I knew it would be too dangerous to hear it. I could see the under-current of desire in his face, feel his need rolling from him.

"Yes. Show me the ship."

We stared at each other a beat longer, then he whirled around. I waited long enough for my pulse to slow and followed him.

# ALMI

*W*e made our way down a short set of steps to the main deck of the ship. The glorious solar sails stood huge and proud over us, glittering like liquid metal. Poseidon moved to the railings, and I followed.

"There are crossbows mounted at regular intervals along the ship's rails," he told me, his tone all business. "They refill with bolts made from a similar material as the solar sails. That means the deeper we go, the less light there is and the less ammo we have."

"Like a battery that runs out in the dark."

He threw a small frown over his shoulder at me. "I do not know what a battery is."

"Like a store of power, that runs out when you use it all."

"Then yes."

"How does the ship keep going without light to power the sails?"

This time, when he looked over his shoulder at me, he

wore an expression laced with pride. "This ship is special. She is the only vessel in all Olympus that can switch out her sails to pagos sails."

"Pagos sails?"

"They are powered by the cold."

"And it's cold under the sea?"

"Yes. The lava breaking through the surface in the last Trial was due to us being on the border of the blacksmith god's volcanic realm, but most of the ocean floor is cool. And the depths we will need to go to are extremely cold."

I frowned. I'd had enough of cold water in the Trial on Apollo's realm. "I may need to borrow your toga again," I said.

"With any luck, we will not get wet. I have barely any water magic left, and your magic is air," he said wryly.

"If you have the only ship that can move through water, how will the others get down to Atlantis?"

Poseidon shrugged. "Ceto is a sea monster, so she will have no problems. And Kalypso is a water Titan. She will be able to devise something, I am sure. Polybotes though, I do not know. Giants have strong ties to Hephaestus' forges—he may be able to seek help there." He turned back to the large crossbow mounted on the railing. "To fire, you send your will into the weapon, just as you did to steer the crosswind in the first Trial."

I followed him around the deck of the ship, making a mental note of everything he told me about how it worked. We went through what to do if the sails were damaged, how the enormous harpoon gun on the peaked front of the ship worked, and where all the emergency hatches to get below deck if the haulers weren't working were.

The irony of Poseidon himself teaching me how to control the ship I had originally planned to steal from him was not lost on me as we made our way back up the steps to the bridge.

He spoke as though I would need to know these things in his absence, and such a large part of me wanted to stop him, unwilling to entertain the idea of losing him for any reason. But there was no point. He would feel better if he thought I could operate the ship without him, and the knowledge sure as hell couldn't hurt.

He told me how to brace myself properly when holding the huge ship's wheel, so that it didn't wipe me off my feet if it spun, and he showed me yet another weapon in the back of the bridge, this one more like a freaking cannon.

"The other thing you need to be aware of on the bridge is the pegasus pen."

"The what now?"

He pointed to a gleaming gold metal sigil on the planks, on the left side of the ship. The gold was shaped like a winged horse. He dropped into a crouch, the movement making his shoulders muscles bulge and a shimmy of appreciation work its way through me.

He pressed his fingertips to the metal symbol. "Think of Blue when you touch it," he said. A whirring sounded, and then I saw movement beyond the railings. When I reached them to look over the edge, a whole section of the ship was sliding out, and a small, roofless stable was contained within the section.

"That's amazing!"

"They will sleep and rest there. There are very few instances where they would want to be inside the stable when it is stowed inside the ship, as they are incredibly claustrophobic creatures."

I nodded in understanding. "I can empathize."

"You are claustrophobic?" he asked me.

"I don't like the thought of being trapped."

"Does anyone?"

I gave him a pointed look. "You choose your own walls, mighty one," I said, giving him a mock bow to emphasize my point. "You can go anywhere, do anything. The decision not to lies with you."

Light burned bright in his eyes a moment, then he turned back to the railings. "The last thing above deck is the underwater shield." He moved back to the ship's wheel and pointed at the trident carved into the very center. "Touch that and will for protection from the water. A magical shield will encompass the ship."

"Including the side-stable?"

"Yes."

"Cool."

"You are cold?"

"No, it's a human word for something good."

His frown lifted. "Humans both intrigue and bore me."

"Then you've met the wrong humans. They are far from boring, trust me."

He cocked his head. "If we survive this, will you show me the human world?"

Both his demeanor and the question itself were so un-godlike that I was momentarily stuck for words. He sounded like a normal guy, asking someone out on a date.

He straightened when I failed to answer. "If you still resent me for forcing you to spend so much time there, then I understand."

"No, I just didn't expect you to ask me that."

He paused. "Does that mean you do not resent me?"

I scowled. "Oh, I still resent you. But I guess there were some pretty awesome places in the human world. California was particularly fun." I wondered how much more fun it would be to visit with an almighty water god. The thought of Poseidon in Hawaiian shorts on a surfboard, performing mind-blowing tricks on the waves, made me smile.

"That's the one—." Poseidon started to say, then closed his mouth abruptly.

"The one what?"

A muscle in his jaw ticked as he kept his lips clamped together. When I realized he wasn't going to answer me, I shook my head. "And you say I'm the odd one. Anyway, yes. If we survive this, I'll show you the places I enjoyed in the human world."

"I would like that." The words sounded like they were being dragged from his lips. "I must show you below deck, now."

# ALMI

*O*nce again, I decided not to push the ocean god. If he thought it best to keep what he'd been about to say to himself, there was probably a good reason.

I followed him into the hauler at the back of the bridge. Unlike the one that hung on the outside of the boat, this one moved down the middle, sinking into the planks just like a wooden elevator.

When it reached the bottom, Poseidon broke the slightly awkward silence. "There are two levels down here. The lowest is all weapons and cargo, and the other is cabins and the galley."

"Is the galley the kitchen?"

"Yes." There was no door on the hauler, and he gestured out at the space before us without stepping out of it. "This is the cargo hold."

There were many large wooden crates and peculiar shaped objects covered in sheets. Round porthole windows let in rays of light, but it was still gloomy. Under each porthole window was a cannon, poking through the hull of the ship.

"Do these cannons reload magically too?"

"Yes. And unlike the ones up top, they can fire light and cold powered ammunition."

"So they'll work when we're really deep?"

"They will. And they are controlled by the ship herself. She will defend herself from threat, but you will need to steer her, as she can only fire the weapons, not aim or move herself."

"Okay."

The hauler began to move upward again, taking us to the next level up.

This time, I found myself looking down a long, nicely decorated corridor. Double doors at the end were carved in the shape of a seashell and glimmered with the same mother-of-pearl shine as my sister's skin.

Poseidon stepped out of the hauler and began to stride down the corridor. "These are guest cabins." He gestured at the wooden doors we passed, stopping when he reached one with a large cresting wave painted on it. "This one is the galley."

He pushed the door open, and I peered in.

All the surfaces were a rich, dark wood, and the walls were painted pale blue. There were sinks and counter-tops, knife racks, and cupboards. "Kitchen," I said with a nod. "Got it."

"Can you cook?"

The question was another unexpected one. "Today is an Almi-pop-quiz," I said, looking at him.

"What is a pop quiz?"

I chuckled. "It doesn't matter. Yes. I can cook. My trailer used to be parked near an Italian restaurant and they used to give away all the food they hadn't sold that was going bad. I make mean pasta."

"Then you are cooking on this voyage."

I raised an eyebrow. "We're calling it a voyage now, are we?"

"Any large undertaking on my ship should be called a voyage," he said, his shoulders squaring.

"I prefer voyage to Trial," I said. "Can you cook?"

"Of course."

"Then why am I cooking on this voyage?"

"I am a king." There was a playfulness to his tone, not an arrogance, and I decided to play along.

"Oh, I see." I bent low. "I shall make my king the finest Italian food that has ever passed his lips."

"I do not know what an Italian is, but I look forward to it."

I grinned at him. He stared at me a beat, then turned away. My smile slipped.

"This is the mess room, or dining room." He pushed open another door to reveal a room that looked fit for a king to eat in. Cherrywood paneling lined a space housing a long table, and the portholes along the hull side of the room were lined with gleaming gold rings. Sea creatures were painted across the ceiling in the same style as his throne room, and I instantly wanted to spend time in there.

"It's lovely."

"Yes." He closed the door. "My chambers are there." He pointed to the double doors at the end. "You may stay in this room." He pointed to a different door at the left end of the corridor, which presumably shared a wall with his.

I moved past him and pushed open the door.

It was nice; a small neat single bed against one wall, two small porthole windows letting in light, and a chest filled with sheets and what looked like shirts. The walls were the same pale blue as the galley. There was a door that I assumed led to a bathroom.

"You know, a gentleman would give the lady the bigger room," I said, stepping back into the corridor and eyeing the huge doors to his room.

He said nothing, but the muscle in his jaw ticked again.

"Since we're having a tour, I'd better see your room too."

Before he could stop me, I pushed the doors to his room open.

"Whoa."

The room was at the front of the ship, so it was a V-shape, and it took up the *whole* of the front of the ship. Instead of porthole windows, enormous full height picture windows lined the back walls. A bed in the shape of a clamshell stood grandly in the center of the room, and somehow managed to look classy, rather than tacky. I stepped into the room, turning in a slow circle. The ceiling, unsurprisingly now, was painted with a beautiful coral scene, turtles, merfolk, dolphins, whales, seahorses, and hippocampi flitting about amongst the underwater garden.

Along the back wall of the room, on either side of the door, were tall bookcases covered with ornaments, small statues and books. A door led to what must have been the room opposite mine in the corridor. A bathroom? I walked to it and pushed it open.

Bathroom didn't come close. It was an indoor beach. Soft white sand covered the floor that wasn't taken up by what had to be described as a pool, rather than a bathtub. The far wall was a waterfall, water running from a split in the wall into the sparkling green pool. Shining mirrors alternated with large windows, reflecting the bright light around the room. It didn't smell of soap, like a normal bathroom, but of the sea, fresh and inviting.

I gaped at Poseidon. "Can I at least have a bath in here?"

His eyes darkened, his jaw working as he dropped his head. "If you remove your clothing in this room, I will not be held responsible for my actions," he growled.

Color leapt to my cheeks and I swallowed. My hands itched to pull my shirt straight off. But that was a bad idea, and we both knew it.

"This is a nice room," I said dumbly instead.

"Would you like it?" he ground out.

I blinked at him. "Who the hell is answering no to that?"

"I have not offered my quarters to anyone my entire, long, life. So I do not know who is saying no to that."

I tried to find some amusement in his tone, but he was a seven-foot tower of tightly coiled energy, and I was getting the distinct feeling that if I pushed him much further, he might explode. "Why are you offering it to me then?"

"You are my wife."

My heart skipped a beat. *Wife*. I'd been his wife my whole adult life, but I'd never actually been treated as such. I looked back at the bed, then at him.

"I don't know if you'll fit in the single bed in the other room."

His eyes flashed. "You misunderstand me. I did not offer to swap rooms with you."

Heat swirled through me on a low, long swoop. "You mean... share?"

I looked back at the enormous bed covered in rich navy silk sheets. Vivid images filled my head, us in the pool together, his whole glorious body on show, me lying back on the bed, his magnificent form towering over me.

"Yes. I mean share."

"Is that a good idea?" My voice was a hoarse whisper.

"No."

"Right."

My face heated so much it was uncomfortable. I turned and walked deliberately past him, to the open doors to his rooms. "I need some air."

"That *is* a good idea."


I headed for the hauler at the other end of the corridor, and only noticed when I reached it that Poseidon hadn't followed me. I saw him disappear into the galley and was relieved.

When I got to the top deck, the cool ocean air calmed

the heat that had been taking over my body. Sharing a room with him wasn't just a bad idea, it was freaking dangerous. My mind skipped gleefully back to how he had made me feel in Aphrodite's palace, causing some of the heat to return instantly to my face. And south of my belly

I could be in serious danger of falling in love with him, I thought ruefully.

If I was being honest with myself though, the gentle questions he'd been asking me that suggested he genuinely wanted to get to know me were just as dangerous.

Distance.

We may have been stuck on the ship together, our goals intricately intertwined and our destinies hand in hand, but I had to keep as much distance as I could between myself and the ticking timebomb that was my husband.

# ALMI

ootsteps made me turn from where I was leaning on the railing. Poseidon came toward me, holding two steaming mugs, and held one out to me.

"Thank you." He just nodded. "How long is the voyage down to Atlantis?" I asked him, trying to stay focused on the practical.

"Two days."

"I read something about sea monsters guarding the route."

He looked grave as he leaned against the railing next to me. "Yes. Two of the most dangerous creatures to inhabit the seas." My stomach squished in apprehension.

"The most dangerous? Worse than the talontaur?" I'd heard stories growing up of the most monstrous sea creatures in Poseidon's seas, and some of them had kept me and my vivid imagination awake at night.

"Worse than the talontaur," Poseidon said. I looked at him, dread forming now in my gut as images from my childhood nightmares flashed before me. *Please don't say-*

"Scylla and Charybdis."

"Fuck," I said on a breath. "And you can't control them?"

"Not without my trident."

The heat that had been engulfing me vanished, replaced by icy fear. I gripped the warm mug, and took a sip. Cinnamon filled my mouth and chased away some of the cold.

"You know these monsters though, right? That must give us some sort of advantage?"

"I designed them, with Ceto and her brother."

"Good. So, you must know their weaknesses?"

He gave a dry snort. "They do not have weaknesses." He straightened suddenly, frowning. "That's not actually true." His words were slow and thoughtful, and I could practically see the cogs turning. "They hate each other."

"Why?"

"What do you know about them?"

"Only what I was told by my sister when I was little."

"Which was?"

"They are so terrifying that people go mad when they encounter them. Scylla is a six-headed sea dragon, and Charybdis is a giant whirlpool with a meat grinder at the bottom."

Poseidon quirked a brow. "Meat grinder is not a bad analogy. Charybdis is more like a giant worm, with a circular mouth and hundreds of layers of teeth. The pull of his whirlpool is enormous, and once you are in his grasp it is near impossible to get out."

"And Scylla? Is he really a six-headed dragon?"

"Yes. *She* has six heads, all on long necks, a mane of lethal spiked horns and a jaw full of teeth on each."

"Obviously," I muttered, and took another sip of cinnamon tea. "When I was a kid, Scylla and Charybdis were used to make a point of learning about having to make hard decisions."

"Yes. The two creatures are rarely separated and were designed to guard passageways. The person wishing to get through must travel close to one of the monsters, and the passageway will be too narrow to avoid them both. They must choose what they believe to be the lesser of two evils."

Another stab of irony clouted me. *Learning to choose between the lesser of two evils. Killing my sister or killing a whole realm.* I looked away from Poseidon, staring over the edge of the ship to the water below. "Meat grinder or multi-headed dragon. Which is worse?"

"In our situation, I do not know. But, Scylla's body is fused to a mountain, far below sea level. Charybdis, though tethered to Scylla, can be moved. With an effort."

"You think we can separate them enough to get through the middle?"

Poseidon shook his head, and a dangerous gleam filled his eyes. "I think we try to do the opposite. I think we try to move Charybdis toward Scylla."

"Let them fight while we scoot past?"

"It would be the fight of centuries," he murmured, and he sounded regretful.

"You're worried they will hurt each other?"

"No, I'm sorry I will not be able to see it if we pull this

off. They are some of the most magnificent killing machines in Olympus."

Poseidon really had led a different life than the one I had. Glee at watching two lethal monsters kill each other was really more of an all-powerful, ancient-god thing than it was an Almi thing.

He glanced at me when I said nothing. "They'll be reborn if they are killed in battle," he said, clearly trying to reassure me.

"Oh. Erm, good."

Once again, Poseidon had been thinking about the repercussions of his actions. I wondered if forcing the monsters to fight would have been a viable strategy for him if they didn't come back to life if they died. I had a feeling the answer was no.

"It will take a great deal of your power to move a monster like Charybdis." Poseidon looked into my eyes, serious and stern. "Do you think you can do it? I am not sure how much I will be able to assist."

I swallowed, trying to decide how truthful to be with him. After a moment's thought, I opted for full honesty. There wasn't any point in lying. If he felt even half as connected to me as I did to him, he would know. "I won't fully embrace my power."

His face didn't change. I didn't even see the telltale flicker of bright blue in his eyes that often gave away his emotions. "How much power do you think you can call on without embracing it fully?"

"I have no idea," I shrugged. His lack of anger or disappointment at my confession was unnerving me. "I expected you to give me a lecture."

"Would you like one?"

"No."

"I can't control your decisions, Almi. Only my own." He looked away from me. "I will not be the one to tell you to cause your sister's death."

Gratitude swamped me, along with a healthy dose of relief. He wasn't going to try to talk me into taking my power. Not even to save his own life, or his realm.

Fresh guilt began to invade the relief. "I'm not refusing to find the Heart of the Ocean or anything," I said quickly. "I'm not giving up. I just think there must be another way, and I won't risk Lily's life until I know there isn't."

He met my eyes again. "One step at a time. We will win these Trials. And then we will cure this blight."

I held my mug out. "To winning the Poseidon Trials."

After a beat, he held his own out and chinked it against mine in a toast. "To winning the Poseidon Trials," he repeated, and we both drank.

When Atlas' voice rang out around us an hour later, my nerves were a jangle of restless knots. "To the starting line, competitors!" There was a flash of light, and the whole ship was transported.

We were hovering over an expanse of clear ocean, and in front of us, lounging on a throne on a marble platform floating high enough for us to see him clearly, was Atlas. He was massive, almost the same size as Polybotes the giant. He was wearing gleaming gold armor from neck to toe, and flames licked over the metal at irregular intervals.

His eyes were bright red, and his dark hair was topped with an elaborate gold headdress made up of interlocking rings.

"Let us recap the scores! Kalypso got one shell in the last Trial and now has ten." High above us a vessel flashed into existence. It was a ship very similar in shape and size to Poseidon's, but it was made of alternating sections of black metal and water. I could see straight through large parts of the hull, and actual fish were swimming around in the watery walls.

"That's frigging awesome," I breathed.

Poseidon frowned at me. "You are not supposed to be impressed by the enemy."

"She has a ship made out of water," I said, looking at him. "There's no scenario in which that's not cool."

He rolled his eyes, but he didn't actually look annoyed.

Kalypso's ship vanished, and Ceto took its place, enlarged so much she was as big as a frigging house. Her tentacles whipped at the air, her soulless black eyes looking over our ship as the red liquid ran like rivers over her leathery flesh. "Ceto is our current leader with eleven shells."

I pulled a face as she vanished, and Polybotes appeared instead. He was standing in a round metal sphere, not a great deal larger than he was. Strips of the sphere were made of glass, like the segments of an orange, and the ball appeared to be equipped with coiled chains and at least two crossbow-style weapons. "The giants in the forges have indeed assisted him," Poseidon muttered.

"They made him that?" I gaped at Poseidon and he nodded.

"It looks like their work. He'd better hope it can withstand the depths." The sea god didn't sound all that convinced that it would.

"Polybotes managed an impressive three shells in the last Trial and has eight overall."

The next flash took me utterly by surprise. The ship and Poseidon vanished around me, reappearing where the other contestants had, high above the ocean surface.

I, on the other hand, stayed exactly where I was. It took less than a second for me to plummet into the freezing waves. I had time to gulp in a breath, and then I was kicking my legs, trying to ignore the shock of the cold and my blistering rage, as I swam back up to the surface. I heard Atlas' voice as my head broke the waves.

"Poseidon has yet to score a single shell."

I looked up and saw Blue's distinct wings as he dove off the edge of the ship, making straight for me. He didn't get far, though, before there was another flash, and the ship and I swapped places.

"Lastly, we have Almi, who appears not to have a vessel to travel to the sunken city of Atlantis in!" Atlas' voice was mocking as I found myself suspended high over the ocean, and Poseidon's ship.

A tingle of panic ran through me, both at the sheer height I was dangling at, but also at the thought that I wouldn't be able to share Poseidon's ship. After all, we were technically competing with one another.

Blue charged through the sky toward me, ducking under me as Atlas' voice rang out again. "Almi is second to last, with nine shells. And it now seems she is traveling to the bottom of the sea on a pegasus." He actually laughed this time, and Blue let out an angry whinny as whatever was holding me in place in mid-air vanished, and I slipped awkwardly as I tried to right myself on his back.

"Thank you, Blue," I said as I gripped his mane. I knew the pegasus' anger was directed at the asshole Titan and not me.

"Let the final Trial commence!"

## ALMI

*B*lue tucked in his wings and dove. I expected him to make for Poseidon's ship, but instead, he angled straight at the surface of the sea. I sent out a silent plea to air for the breathing bubbles and held my breath for the second time.

I was more prepared for the cold as we plunged under the water. Bubbles zoomed toward me, wrapping around my head and filling my mouth with air as Blue spread out his wings and gave them a hard beat. I could feel his legs kicking hard under us, and we kept moving deeper.

As the air before my eyes settled, I twisted my head and watched as the other competitors sank in their various vessels around me. Kalypso's distinctive black panels were the most obvious, and she was still closest to the surface. Polybotes' sphere was sinking steadily, and Ceto's inky form was already far below me. Poseidon's ship was at the same level as Blue.

The front was tipped forward slightly, the gleaming gold sails slicing through the water. Poseidon was standing at the helm, gripping the wheel, and the sight of him made my breath catch.

He was magnificent. His white hair billowed behind him in the water, and the light rippling through the water and reflecting off the sails played across his solid chest.

As I watched, the color of the light changed, the gleaming liquid gold sails darkening. As though navy ink had been poured down them, the gold melted away, and they reminded me of a breathtaking night sky, covered in glittering stars. They still looked as though the material was made of liquid metal, but now deep and rich and dark.

A bubble started to grow from the middle mast as I stared, expanding into a dome just like the ones that covered the cities in Aquarius, a slight golden shimmer to it. Poseidon moved his head, locking his eyes on me. Without a word from me, Blue shifted, and we powered toward the ship.

Blue slipped through the shield with no resistance at all, and I let out a heavy breath of relief. He landed on the main deck, and my bubbles pulled away from my face to form the little whirlwind.

"Thank the gods for that," I muttered, as I slid from Blue's back. "And thank the gods for you." I patted Blue's haunches, and he stamped his feet before spreading his wings and shaking them. I squealed as water covered me from head to foot. My whirlwind rushed me, spinning around me in a flash, lifting my hair and pulling my shirt from my belt. I squealed again as it spun me around, spluttering a laugh as I realized it had almost dried me completely.

"And thank you too!" It zoomed around my head, just half a foot high again. Tucking my shirt back in, I set off for the bridge at a jog.

"You know, I worried Atlas was going to find a way to keep us separated," I said to Poseidon as I stepped off the last step and onto the bridge.

He didn't look at me, and I frowned and sped up. "Everything okay?"

"The ship," he ground out.

"Your face," I murmured, coming to a stop next to him. *Stone.* So much stone. "What's wrong with the ship?"

"When you and Blue landed, it all but stopped responding to me. It's taking everything I have to keep her on course."

"Atlas," I said in a hiss. "He *has* found a way to try to keep us apart."

Poseidon gave me a very brief sideways glance. "He could not interfere with my ship."

"Are you sure?"

"Yes. It would be like interfering with Chrysos or Blue."

"Then maybe the ship just doesn't like me." I laid my hand on the wheel next to his, and felt the vessel judder underneath me.

Poseidon's eyes snapped to mine. "You are right. She does not trust you." His own eyes darkened briefly, as though he wondered if that meant he shouldn't trust me either.

I released the wheel and put my hand over the top of Poseidon's instead.

*Can you hear me?* I asked the ship.

We jerked again.

*I'm going to take that as a yes. We're going to need you to put on the performance of your life today. Poseidon's life, trident and realm are dependent on it.*

An image flashed into my head, unbidden. It was dark and disconnected, but I saw myself, I saw golden snakes, and I saw Poseidon on his knees, stone covering his body.

I was so shocked I pulled my hand from Poseidon's. "Did you see that?"

"See what?"

"I think the ship just showed me something."

Poseidon's face creased thoughtfully. "She is powerful, and the ships have mental connections. I suppose it is possible. What did you see?"

"Something that hasn't happened."

"No. That is not possible."

I heard Kryvo's voice, small and I was fairly sure only for me. "Put me on the wheel. I can feel the ship, a bit like the statues in the palace."

I lifted him from my collar and laid him on the wood. His little tentacles wrapped around a spoke.

"What are you doing?" Poseidon looked at me and I waved a hand at him.

"Starfish stuff."

"We are losing speed. We need to do something."

"I'm trying to."

Kryvo spoke again. "She does not like you. She believes that you will be the cause of Poseidon's death."

"What? How? Why?" The questions came out one after another, and Poseidon looked at Kryvo, then me.

"She doesn't know any of those things, only that you are a bad omen for her king."

I ground my teeth. "He's supposed to be the cause of my damned death!" I protested. "Not the other way around!"

Poseidon fell so still next to me that, for a second, I worried he may have turned to stone again. I looked at his face and saw he had closed his eyes.

"Is he talking to the ship?" I whispered to Kryvo.

"I think so," the starfish whispered back.

After a minute that felt like a freaking hour, I felt the ship start to speed up. When Poseidon opened his eyes, we were moving at almost twice the speed we had been. He reached for my hand, and I let him take it. Studiously ignoring the zing of electricity that shot between us, he wrapped my fingers around the spoke of the wheel. "Almi, meet *Mossy*."

I felt a flash of heat under my fingertips. *Hi. I'm not trying to kill your king. I promise.*

The heat cooled instantly, and the same image I'd seen before popped into my head. I tried to hold onto it, to make out more detail than I'd seen last time, but it was just as fragmented as it was before. Just as it slipped away though, I thought I saw myself lying on the ground at Poseidon's feet, pale, unmoving, and lifeless.

I let go of the wheel.

"What happened" Poseidon looked at me, concern in his bright eyes.

"I just saw the image again. I thought I saw…" I trailed

off, unwilling to say what I'd seen. "It was weird," I finished lamely. "The ship's moving faster, what did you say to her?"

"How important it was that we win this Trial."

"Good."

I picked up Kryvo and put him back on my collarbone. I didn't know if it was normal that I now craved his reassuring presence, or if that made me even odder than everyone already thought I was.

At this point, I wasn't really sure I cared.

"How long will it take us to get to Scylla and Charybdis?" I asked.

"About a day."

"What?" I stared at him. "A whole day?"

"We are going deeper than most minds can comprehend."

"Oh. So… We *are* going to have to choose a bedroom at some point."

He looked at me. "There are many creatures guarding the deep. I suggest one of us stays on watch at all times."

"Good idea. Maybe we can build a blanket-fort up here."

He blinked. "A blanket-fort? Is this a human thing?"

"No, Lily and I built blanket-forts all the time."

"Explain this fort-building to me."

His grip on the ship's wheel had relaxed, and I was confident *Mossy* was doing most of the work now. "You get a load of sheets, a couple chairs, cushions, some snacks and a drink, and you build a fort," I said.

He cocked his head, thinking. "A furniture fortress?"

I laughed. "That sounds like an upgrade. But yes. Exactly that. If you have fairy lights, then you're acing it."

He considered me a moment. "You would rather sleep in a structure made of soft furnishings on the bridge, than in a bedroom?"

"I'd rather sleep anywhere that keeps us close," I said, then felt color rush my cheeks. "For safety, I mean," I added in a rush. "It's all very well for you to keep watch, but without your magic you might need me quickly."

"I concur."

"Really?"

"Yes. You keep watch, and I will gather the necessary equipment."

# ALMI

*W*atching the god of the sea, one of the three ruling Kings of Olympus, and the most serious man I'd ever met, build a fortress out of cushions was a frigging delight.

And it was an excellent blanket-fort. Or more accurately, a fortress. He'd brought up four of the overly grand dining chairs, a whole load of sheets, and armfuls of cushions over three feet wide.

"Are those from your bed?" I asked him as he arranged a series of smaller black velvet cushions across the back of the makeshift mattress.

"Everything is from my bed," he grunted from inside the fort.

Lily shimmered into being in my head. *Almi, I know I said I wouldn't get involved with you two, but you do realize sleeping with him up here is the same as sleeping with him in his bed, right? I only mention it because if you fall in love with him, you'll die. And then so will he and all of Aquarius.*

*Jeez, not much pressure then,* I replied. *We're taking turns.*

*Don't worry. I'm not falling in love with him. And I'm still not convinced he loves me.*

Her face did that thing where she was clearly about to say something and thought better of it it. *Fine. Keep it that way.*

*I will.*

*Good. Know that if you don't, and you two get too close, you're going to get me popping up in your head. I'll do whatever takes to keep my baby sister safe.*

I groaned out loud and Poseidon turned from where he was kneeling in the den. "Am I doing it wrong?"

"No. No, you're doing great."

*Lily, I'm not going to get too close to him. I swear.*

*Good.*

I turned to face the darkening water around us as my sister's face vanished from my mind. As we got deeper, less light penetrated the ocean, and there was something unsettling about the endless inky gloom. We'd lost sight of the other ships a long time ago, though we had seemed to be ahead of Polybotes and Kalypso, and behind Ceto.

"What happens if we get to the sea monsters after everyone else?" I asked.

Poseidon appeared beside me, startling me. "The fortress is ready."

"Oh. Right." I turned and dropped to my knees at the entrance to the makeshift tent, dutifully admiring his handiwork. "It's lovely," I told him. He frowned.

"It is adequate?"

"Yes."

"As good as you made as a child?"

I paused as I looked at the beautiful wood of the chairs, and the rich velvet cushions. "It's fancier," I said.

"Is that good?"

I sat down on the mattress he'd made, swivelling on my butt to look at him. He was bent over and looking at me anxiously. My heart swelled a little at the sight.

"Why are you so keen to do a good job?"

He paused, then said, "A king takes pride in all his tasks."

"Right."

"And you are a queen."

My heart skipped a beat. "It's as good as when I was a kid," I confirmed.

He looked satisfied as he dropped down to the planks, drawing his knees up and resting his muscular arms across them.

"If the others reach the monsters before us, we may be lucky. They may remove them from our path."

"Are any of them strong enough to do that?"

"Ceto and Kalypso might be."

"If we lose, who would be the best and worst to win in our place?"

He gave me a dark look. "We will not lose."

"Uh-huh. But if we do."

I thought he wouldn't answer me, but then he spoke. "Kalypso would be my preference to win."

"Really?"

"She is the only one who might challenge Atlas. I don't believe that she would hand my realm over to him."

I thought about the hunger in her eyes when she'd

cornered me in the dining hall. "I agree. Why do you think they are all competing for him?"

"He'll have bargained with them or blackmailed them. Polybotes might just be competing for his own revenge."

"Dare I ask what you did to him?"

"I am the creator of all giants. He has not agreed with all of my decisions."

I decided to ask him to elaborate later, not that I figured he would actually tell me anymore about his history with the giant.

"What do you think he's got on Ceto?"

"She will have been the easiest to bring around." I could hear the anger in his voice immediately. "If he offered her freedom in exchange for the realm if she wins, then she will not have hesitated."

"She scares the living shit out of me," I said.

He glanced at me. "She is designed to do just that. Her brother is worse, though he is incredibly stupid." He let out a long sigh. "We combined our magic to create incredible creatures - Scylla and Charybdis included. I am disappointed, though not surprised, that she has broken our tenuous bond."

For some unfathomable reason, hearing him talk about a bond to someone else, even a woman who was half rotten sea monster, made me irritable. "And Kalypso?" I asked. "What do you think he has on her?"

"I wish I knew. She has power and a place of privilege in Aphrodite's realm."

"Why is she not a part of your realm if she is a water goddess?"

"When the Titans lost the war, she asked me for a

place in Aquarius. Her father is Oceanus, the most powerful water god to have ever existed. He fought against his own kind in the war, helping the Olympians. Zeus spent a long time trying to make Titan descendants unwelcome in Olympian society, and he wouldn't allow me to accept someone as strong as Kalypso in my palace."

More irritation flowed through me at the idea of Kalypso living in Poseidon's palace, but I shoved it down. "Did that piss her dad off?"

"Yes. Oceanus removed himself from Olympus. It is my belief that he caused all the other primordial Titans to disappear."

"And Kalypso went to Aphrodite?"

"Aphrodite went to her," he corrected me. "Kalypso is beautiful, fierce and powerful. Just the sort of friend Aphrodite likes at court."

"Why didn't Zeus stop Aphrodite like he did you?"

Poseidon snorted. "Stop the goddess of love from doing what she wanted? You are aware of my almighty brother's reputation with women?"

I nodded. "I heard it wasn't just women."

"You heard right. Zeus will put his dick in anything that moves."

"Huh. So Aphrodite seduced him?"

"She seduced him every few months, whenever she wanted something."

Fresh irritation rolled through me, and I cursed this new jealous streak that had risen up out of nowhere as my mouth opened without my permission. "Did she ever seduce you?"

His eyes snapped to mine. "No."

"Oh."

A tense silence descended, and I pretended to inspect my nails for dirt.

"Do you want to sleep now, or take the first watch?" Poseidon asked eventually.

"As I'm already in the fortress, I guess I'll sleep now, if that's okay with you?"

"Good. I will wake you in three hours or so." He stood up and disappeared from my view.

I flopped back onto the cushions with a heavy breath. Just spending time around him was starting to feel dangerous. Every minute, every sentence, every flash of emotion made me warm to him more. And worse, made me doubt my insistence that he didn't have feelings for me.

# ALMI

*I* slept fitfully, but my grogginess when Poseidon woke me vanished fast. When I crawled out of the tent, clutching Kryvo on his little cushion, the sea god was waiting with a plate covered in hot bacon and toast. I stretched, then took the plate from him.

"Thank you. I thought I was cooking pasta?"

"I heard this meat was popular with humans."

"You found bacon just for me?"

"*Mossy* did."

"The ship?"

"Yes."

"How? Has she decided she doesn't hate me yet?"

Poseidon turned to the railings. It was really dark around us now, the only light coming from the gentle glow of the shield over us. "She can conjure whatever food is required. She is no normal ship."

I decided not to point out that he had ignored my second question. "I read about her, in my book. She sounds very special."

He rubbed his hand along the wood fondly. "She is."

"Anything happen while you were on watch?" I moved to the wheel, reluctant to touch the wood myself, lest I be bombarded with more weird images.

"No. I think we are about six hours away now."

"Good. You need more rest than me, according to Persephone. You should sleep as long as you can."

I expected him to argue, or try to be all proud and testosterone-y, but he surprised me by nodding. "Agreed. The more I sleep now, the more I may be of use in battle."

Sensible guy. Of course.

"Enjoy the fortress," I said as he dropped to his knees and crawled inside.

"Wake me if anything happens." I heard his deep voice from under the sheet.

"I will."

I sat down on the deck, leaning my back against the railings and plopping Kryvo's cushion down in front of me so that I could tuck into my bacon and toast. "Did you get any sleep, Kryvo?" I asked around a mouthful of salty deliciousness.

"Yes. A little."

"Good."

"Almi?"

"Uh-huh?" I swallowed my too-large mouthful.

"I am worried."

"You and me both, little friend."

"I'm serious."

"So am I." I set down my empty plate, then gently lifted the starfish onto my palm. "What's wrong?"

"I do not see how you can face Medusa and survive."

"I don't plan to face her," I told him. "I plan to do exactly what you would tell me to do and hide from her."

"You do?" he said hopefully.

"Yes. If Poseidon knows of no way for me to survive her stare, then I'd be an idiot to do anything else."

"Do you think she will be in Atlantis?"

"Yes. But I'm more worried about getting to Atlantis right now." I stood up as I spoke, turning to look out into the dark beyond. The ship was still tilted slightly downward at the front, but for the most part we were just sinking into the depths. I didn't even want to know how much distance there was between us and the surface. The thought made my chest tight.

"Scylla and Charybdis?" asked Kryvo.

"Yeah. Hopefully, the others will get there first and deal with them." I was only half joking.

"They will not harm Ceto. She is their mother."

"Hmmm. She's supposed to have given up all familial advantage," I said doubtfully.

"Would you like to see them? There are a few paintings in the palace I could show you."

I considered his offer as I stared out into the dark. Part of me thought I should be prepared. The other part thought that if I knew what we were about to face I'd want to turn and run. Only, there was nowhere to run.

"Tell me about them, instead," I said. "Anything you think might be helpful."

"Okay." The little starfish sounded less frightened, now

he had something to do. "Scylla's body is fused to a mountain, and she can't move. She has six long necks that look like they can bend in any direction, and each head has a long thin jaw with lots of teeth. In both images of her I can see, she is picking prey off the deck of ships with her multiple heads."

"Okay," I said, beginning to regret asking him. A flash of light in the dark blue beyond made me pause. "Hold on a moment, Kryvo," I whispered. "What was that?"

The light flashed again, then again. I stared as a creature drifted into view. It was huge, about half the size of our ship, but I knew instantly that it meant us no harm.

"It's a hippocampus," said Kryvo. "But not like the ones you get in Aquarius."

He was right. The hippocampi in Aquarius were like seahorses crossed with actual horses, their tails curled up and round, but with the heads and front legs of a stallion. They were usually blue or green.

This creature, though... It too had the curled tail of a seahorse and the head and top-torso of a horse, but it was almost white. Lights, intensely bright blue, flashed all along it in quick pulses. The mane flowing from its massive head was rippling with silver light, and its eyes were the same color, bright and filled with intelligence.

"It's beautiful."

"And deadly."

I was starting to believe that most beautiful things were deadly. "Tell me about Charybdis," I said as it drifted out of view.

"There are more pictures of Charybdis, including an image of when he nearly ate Persephone."

"What?"

"Persephone faced the Hades Trials, and she had to collect a gemstone whilst riding a hippocampus and avoiding being sucked into Charybdis' mouth."

"Well," I said, a little stunned. "If we survive this, I'll be wanting to hear that story."

"It proves that what Poseidon said was true — Charybdis is the one that can be moved."

"Does he just look like a whirlpool?"

"If the whirlpool had a massive worm mouth with many rings of teeth at the bottom, then yes."

"Right."

An hour passed by, and I became increasingly more restless, sitting on the deck with nothing but my anxiety and many unanswered questions to concentrate on. "Do you know any stories, Kryvo?"

"There are many in the palace."

"Could you tell me one? Preferably one with happy ending."

"I shall look for something appropriate," he said.

When five and a half hours had passed, and I'd raided the galley twice for more helpings of bacon, I crouched in front of the blanket-fort.

"Poseidon?"

He sat up immediately, hand moving to the knife at his side. He relaxed as he saw me.

"Did you sleep in all that stuff?" All his leather strapping was still across his chest. I blushed as I realized I was openly staring at his pecs.

"Yes."

"Right. Did you sleep okay?"

"Yes."

"Would you like some bacon?"

He paused. "Yes."

Poseidon ate, and I told him about the hippocampus we'd seen. His eyes turned wistful as I spoke.

"They are truly magnificent creatures. You are fortunate to have seen one."

"I felt fortunate," I told him. "How will we know when we are close?"

Before he could answer me, the ship jerked beneath us. Poseidon moved fast, laying his hand on the ship's wheel when he reached it.

"We are close," he said drily.

I peered out over the railings and saw that there was light coming from beneath us. It was blue, nothing like the warm glow of the shield, and it flashed and moved. We continued our descent until I could see solid rock. "Is that the ocean floor?"

"Yes."

The pale blue light was beaming up from cracks in the rock, which widened out into a river of icy light, flowing faster than the ocean water it was submerged in. It formed an illuminated path that lit the side of a massive, dark mountain on our left.

"Is that the mountain Scylla is attached to?" I whispered.

"It's a dormant volcano, but yes." The ship leveled out, and began to follow the river of light.

As soon as we rounded the mountain, I got my first glimpse of the two legendary sea monsters.

Scylla was indeed fused to the mountainside, as Poseidon had said. Snaking out from the rock were six long necks, covered in gleaming barbs. A tail protruded from the rock too, swinging back and forth, its reach as long as the neck's. The heads on the end of each neck made my legs feel weak. The jaws were abnormally long, clearly designed to stab between sails on ships, picking off prey exactly as Kryvo had described. The teeth lining each jaw were so huge the mouths didn't close properly. Worse, each head was easily the size of a car.

Charybdis was lower than the other monster, the whirlpool part of him set into the ground on the opposite side of the river. But poking up out of the middle of the whirlpool was the ugliest, most grotesque-looking worm I'd ever seen. The whole thing's head was a mouth, circular and lined with layer after layer of needle-sharp teeth.

The monsters were lit by the eery, pale blue, flickering light of the river, and the ocean around us was impenetrably black. The gap between the two colossal creatures was barely bigger than the ship, but on the other side, rippling with silver light, was a round portal.

"Air, I'm gonna need some serious help, here," I muttered.

# ALMI

My little whirlwind zoomed about excitedly. "It's alright for you, you're not about to get eaten by sea monsters," I muttered. It stilled, as though trying to show me it could be serious. "Are you ready to kick some sea monster butt?"

It bounced up and down.

"I'm going to need you to be about ten times bigger, and seriously strong. Think you can do that?"

It bounced again.

"And I'm also going to need you to not kill my sister. You got it?"

It hesitated, then bounced again, not quite as vigorously as before. I got the distinct impression the hesitation was due to doubt, rather than an actual desire to harm Lily.

"Look." Poseidon's deep voice caught my attention, and I followed his pointing arm.

Kalypso.

Her black and water ship was hovering right near the

river, and it looked as though she was either unable or unwilling to move between the two creatures. *Mossy* dropped lower, moving closer to the Titan's ship, and I saw a huge tear in the black metal part of the hull, as though a tooth had dragged clean through the metal.

"Poseidon!" Her voice boomed through the water, echoing with a gurgling sound. "Almi!"

"What do we do?" I asked Poseidon. Our ship slowed to a stop beside hers. She was standing on the bridge. There was no shield keeping the water out of her way, and it made me wonder briefly why Poseidon had one. After all, he could breathe underwater as easily as he could breathe on land.

"You will not be able to pass," Kalypso called before Poseidon could answer my question.

"You don't know that," I called back.

"We stand a better chance working together."

I raised my eyebrows in surprise. "She wants to work together?" I hissed at Poseidon.

He turned to me, his voice low. "She can't get past alone."

"Then we should take advantage and leave her here, surely?"

Doubt flickered over his face. "Almi... I have no question that your magic is strong. But you will not embrace it all." I frowned, wanting to protest but not sure I could. "And besides, if we manage to pull off our plan and force the two monsters to fight each other, she will be just as able to sail past them as we will."

I screwed up my face. He was right. Our plan would remove the monsters from *everyone's* path. If we couldn't use Poseidon's power, then the addition of a water Titan's magic might be more helpful than I wanted to admit. I thought about what Poseidon had said earlier, about Kalypso being the only one of the competitors who might not give up the realm of Aquarius to Atlas if she were to win. "Fine," I said.

We both turned to Kalypso. "I want to move Charybdis," called Poseidon.

Kalypso leaped off the bridge of her ship and darted through the water toward us, so fast it took me by surprise. Clearly Poseidon had the same thought because his knife was in his hand in a flash.

"I am not here to fight you," Kalypso said as she reached the edge of our shield, just a few feet away from us. Her watery hair caught the icy light, her dark skin almost giving off its own glow. She was truly magnificent under the water; it was where she belonged. "Did you just say you wish to *move* Charybdis?"

"Yes. Pit the two creatures against each other. I believe it is the only way to distract them."

Kalypso nodded slowly. "Yes. I like this plan." She looked at me. "Having been on the receiving end of your blustery friend, I know your strength." She glared at my little whirlwind, and it zoomed around my head, taunting her.

"Between us, we should be able to do this," I said, keeping my shoulders squared and my voice confident.

"Agreed." She looked back to Poseidon. "And you? Will you be adding your now-less-than-considerable abilities to this quest?"

"I shall steer my ship," he ground out. I couldn't

imagine he was enjoying admitting he could do nothing to help.

A strange wail rippled through the water, and we all turned our heads to look at the source. Scylla's heads all ducked and turned to us, the blue light of the river lighting them from beneath. As one, the six jaws opened, and I shuddered as the wail sounded again. Forked tongues flicked out between the too-big teeth, and as they moved the barbs covering each neck flashed, showing themselves to be black and slick with something that caught the light.

In response to the wail was a slicing, gnashing sound that was so high-pitched it made my head hurt. The hideous-looking worm thing that was Charybdis was rising out of the spinning whirlpool, its round mouth vibrating in the water.

"Are they communicating with each other?" asked Kalypso.

"I don't know. But let's not waste any more time."

"I concur. Are you ready, land-lover?" She looked at me and I scowled.

"Land-lover?"

"You have no affinity with water. I can tell that even from spending very little time with you."

"Air-lover might be more accurate, then," I said, trying not to let her words get to me. They were true, and I'd known it my whole life, but that didn't change the years of wishing they weren't. I was a sea nymph, for god's sake, I was supposed to have a connection to the water.

Kalypso rolled her eyes. "I am bored with this. It is

time to show the world what I am made of." She held up her hands, and the water around them began to churn.

"Come on, air, let's show this jumped-up Titan we're just as good as she is," I said to my whirlwind. It bounced, then flew through the shield.

For a moment, I thought it might try to combine itself with Kalypso's magic, as it had with Poseidon's to get us under the lavafall. But even the thought of combining my magic with hers made an uneasy sensation roll in my gut, and the whirlwind flew straight past the Titan, toward Charybdis.

I swallowed, nerves and fear twisting inside me. I had no idea how what I was doing.

"Lift the worm out of its hole," said Poseidon. "Then throw it at Scylla."

I looked at the grotesque flailing worm that could have swallowed my trailer whole.

"Easy," I muttered.

I projected my thoughts at my air friend. *We need to lift the worm out of the hole and throw it at the dragon heads.*

The whirlwind was growing as it approached Charybdis, and Kalypso's churning water was racing along beside it.

The worm roared when the two magics hit it.

I cried out in both surprise and pain at the sound, clapping my hands over my ears. I felt my connection to the whirlwind slip as my concentration was ruptured, and I forced myself to focus through the discomfort.

*Dig it out of the hole!*

The whirlwind tightened into a spinning rod and dipped between the worm's huge, wavering body and the whirlpool it was housed in. Kalypso's water was wrapping around it like a lasso, and it thrashed even harder.

With a whoosh, my air zoomed back into sight, it too wrapping itself around the worm's body but starting from the bottom of the whirlpool.

"On the count of three," called Kalypso. "One..." My cord of air glistened in the light of the river as it kept tightening itself around the worm. "Two..." Kalypso's shimmering jet of water was now firmly wound around the thing's head too, underneath the gnashing ring of teeth. "Three!"

I sent a blast of mental power at my air, and Charybdis shrieked again as he was jerked a meter out of the whirlpool. I felt a pull myself, my chest tightening and my mind going fuzzy.

"Hold on!" Poseidon's voice was laced with excitement, and that spurred me on. I kept channelling my thoughts, trying to fight back the exhaustion that was overcoming my body.

The worm jerked again, and again, and then he began to move slowly at first, then faster. The pull on my body lessened, and then the creature was free, pulled completely from the spinning water. It thrashed and flailed in the water, and Kalypso shouted again.

"Now!"

*Now*! I repeated the command to the air, and the worm went pelting through the water toward Scylla's waiting jaws.

The second the teeth closed over the worm's body, the

ship moved beneath my feet. Kalypso threw an unreadable glance at me, then she was zooming back to her own ship. My air magic rushed toward us as we raced along the river.

I had no idea how long the two creatures would be distracted by each other, but clearly Poseidon was taking no chances.

I moved from the railings, once my whirlwind was safely back through the shield, and jogged to Poseidon.

"You did well," he said when I reached him at the wheel.

"Air did well," I said.

We had reached the monsters now, and my gaze was drawn to the epic battle. Poseidon had kept the ship low to the river, aiming straight for the center of the portal at the end of it, which meant the monsters towered over the sails of our ship as we sped along. Five of Scylla's heads had the worm in their mouths, and the sixth was snapping at its face. The worm's body dripped with red slime, and the sheer size of the two creatures made my knees weak.

We were almost past them when the sixth head froze. I watched, almost in slow motion as Charybdis' worm head moved in unison with it, snapping to us.

"Poseidon, I think they've seen us." I felt my legs moving me backward, even though backing up would achieve nothing.

"Shit," he swore, and the ship sped up a fraction more.

It wasn't enough though.

Scylla's sixth head dove at us, lightning fast. For a moment, I thought she'd taken a wild and inaccurate stab as the huge jaw slammed into the lower part of the deck, nowhere near where Poseidon and I were standing. Then I heard a loud whinny.

"Blue!" I shrieked. Without hesitation, I sent my whirlwind toward the snapping jaws. This close, I could see Scylla's leathery hide was deep red in color, and the barbs were indeed dripping with something that looked like oil, flecks of it falling onto the planks and sizzling.

My whirlwind was ten feet tall when it reached the head, and it smashed into it with such force that both the head and the ship jolted. It beat against the snapping jaws, and Blue galloped across the deck toward us, away from the head, followed by Chrysos.

There was another shriek, and the ship jerked to a stop. "Poseidon?" I looked at him, panic rising. He looked back at me, then ran to the railings.

Scylla was still holding the worm part of Charybdis in her mouths, but now the giant round worm-mouth was spinning, sucking everything in its path into it. Including us.

There was movement on our right, and Kalypso's ship soared past us. She'd let us go first, which meant the monsters had two chances of being distracted from her, first by each other, then by us.

"Asshole!" I roared at her. She locked eyes with mine, then blasted beyond us.

*Mossy* heaved, but rather than move forward, she was sucked sideways, toward the meat-grinder mouth.

"Air!"

But my whirlwind was still beating against the snapping sixth head of Scylla, and I could see that if it let up for even a moment, we would be dragon food.

"Shit, shit, shit." I whirled on the spot, looking for anything that might help us, as the ship began kept lurching inexorably toward Charybdis' mouth. Debris and rock were flying past us, anything not anchored down sucked into its maw. The ship cannons were firing, but they were either missing their target, or the ammunition was ineffective.

All we'd done was made sure we had to beat both monsters, instead of one, I realized in horror, as the blanket-fort flew past my head.

Poseidon ran back to the wheel, closed his eyes, and yelled for me to hold on to something. I raced to the wheel, too, wrapping my arms around it.

"What about the pegasi?"

"They made it to the stable. I'm closing them inside the ship!" *Mossy* spun abruptly so that the front was facing the churning maw, instead of the bridge. There was a roar that I was sure was Scylla, and I turned my head in time to see it snap at the main mast of the ship. The whirlwind could only do so much without my constant energy and focus driving it, and I felt a stab of terror as the dragon's teeth sank into the wood of the mast. The whole thing creaked loudly, then began to tip.

The mast crashed to the deck, the beautiful sail tangling around it as it fell. The view ahead of us now was clear, and my heart skipped a beat. The front of the ship was just meters from Charybdis' churning teeth and endless black gullet.

# ALMI

"My children." A melodic voice rang through the sounds of our ship being torn apart, and abruptly, everything stilled. The ship stopped moving, Scylla's heads stopped snapping, and the writhing body of Charybdis froze.

Poseidon was the only thing that moved, and he turned, gazing over his shoulder.

I followed his look, and gasped.

Ceto was behind us, and she was easily as big as the two sea monsters. Her octopus half was low to the ocean floor, her tentacles on either side of the river, holding her colossal body above the glowing water.

Her human half somehow looked completely different than it did on dry land.

The blue light played over her red and black skin, and her black eyes were massive as she surveyed the scene. She looked fearsome and regal, rather than grotesque. I found myself wanting to bow to her.

"My children, you are being used."

I held my breath, not daring to even whisper in the silence that had descended, lest our trip into Charybdis' gullet be resumed.

"Consuming the King is not on your list of tasks today. Pray, let us pass, and I will return you to your rightful positions." Her black eyes moved briefly to Poseidon, then back to the monsters.

Slowly, ever so slowly, the other five heads of Scylla let go of Charybdis' body. The ship shuddered beneath us, then stuttered forward, like a car struggling to start.

Poseidon turned to face the sea goddess as the water flashed red around us, and Charybdis vanished. I moved cautiously to the railings. He was back inside the whirlpool, which was whirling to life around his body.

"Why have you saved our lives?" Poseidon called to Ceto, still towering over us all.

A slow smile spread across her face. "A favor here and there can save one's own life," she said. Her voice, so scratchy on land, was beautiful underwater.

Poseidon paused, then bowed his head. "Consider us in your debt," he said.

She gave a low chuckle. "Oh, I do, Sea King."

There was another flash of red, and then she was a third of the size, and hovering right beside our ship. Her voice rang out, but this time it was in my head. *There is more at stake than you know, Sea King and his Queen. When I need the favor returning, I expect you to deliver.*

Then she was gone, zooming toward the portal and vanishing into it.

A low, pained wail came from Scylla at the departure of his mistress.

"We should go, like, now," I said, casting a glance at the six-headed beast.

Poseidon gripped the wheel. "Come on, *Mossy*. I know you've been injured, but it's not far." The ship inched forward, but it was more of a limp than a sprint. Another wail came from Scylla.

"Air? Fancy giving us a jumpstart?" My whirlwind sprang to life beside me, then whooshed outside the shield. It vanished from view, and a second later, the ship began moving.

"Thanks, air!" I hollered, as we began to power toward the portal.

Questions were whirring through my adrenaline-fuelled brain as we reached the swirling mass of silver water that made up the portal, but apprehension, along with sheer exhaustion, stopped me from voicing any of them. I just clung to the railings as the prow of the ship pushed through the portal, and then the rest of us followed.

For a brief moment, there was just swirling water crashing over our shield, but then we broke through the other side. My eyes widened as I took in the scene before us.

About five miles away, gleaming in the dark and resting on the ocean floor, was a city. The dome encompassing it wasn't the soft gold of the domes in Aquarius but a cold white silver, which illuminated the ruins inside. Large temples and a massive palace in the center were crumbled remains of what they must once have been. We were too far away for me to make out anything other than the larger buildings inside.

But it was clearly once a grand place. I looked at Poseidon.

"Is that it? Atlantis?"

"Yes. Save your energy and your magic. *Mossy* will get us there in about half an hour, I think, and we need time to eat and recover."

I nodded, and projected my thoughts to air. *The ship is going to take it from here, have a rest.*

Poseidon turned away from the wheel, and his bright eyes locked on mine.

"Why did Ceto just help us?" I asked him, moving closer.

"She is still loyal to me."

"She's competing against you to win your realm and trident! That hardly seems like loyalty."

"She just saved our lives, Almi. She broke the rules, commanded her brethren, and saved us."

"What was she talking about when she said-"

Poseidon held his hand up, halting me. "She told us in private for a reason," he said, voice low enough that I struggled to hear him from just a few feet away.

"Okay. Well, what did it mean?"

"It means, if we can't win, we help Ceto win. At all costs."

I would have expected to feel uncomfortable at the idea of willing Ceto to win over Kalypso, but the last few minutes had made me think otherwise. "She's pretty fucking impressive underwater," I muttered.

"You should see me at full power."

I looked up at him in surprise, and realized I wasn't the only one feeling the adrenaline rush from our life-and-death battle. He looked alive, that same wildness in his face I'd seen in a few of the Trials.

"I'd like that," I said, before I could stop myself. His eyes darkened with what I was sure was desire, and I gulped. "We just almost died," I said, trying to backpedal.

"Yes. But here we are." His intense, burning gaze kept boring into me.

I grasped for something to say that would douse the intensifying emotion blazing between us. "It's a good thing we don't need *Mossy* for much longer." I gestured at the fallen mast and saw pain cross his face, breaking the spell.

"She can be repaired. But not any time soon." His stare moved and rested on Atlantis. "Almi, if we come across Medusa on our hunt for shells, you must-"

"Run and hide," I cut him off. "I know. I may be odd, but I'm not stupid."

Slowly, he reached his arm out for me. Equally slowly, I stepped forward and took his outstretched hand. He tugged me into him, and I let out a hard breath as an overwhelming feeling of *rightness* engulfed me. His scent, his presence... his everything.

I needed him.

The feeling whacked into me, and when my arm brushed against the stone covering the side of his ribs, a hard lump formed in my throat.

How the hell could I choose between him and my sister? Between him and fucking anything?

# POSEIDON

$\mathcal{I}$t had been more decades than I could recall since the war with the Titans, and the only time I had ever believed my immortal life to be in danger.

Until now. The stone blight was not just slowly killing me; it was making me vulnerable to every threat I faced during the Trials.

But when staring down death at the jaws of a monster of my own creation, I found myself caring nothing for my own life, only for that of the woman now in my arms.

I wanted to tell her so many things. To explain my actions, to ease her frustration.

I nearly had, a dozen times.

The need to tell her how I truly felt, to say those three words to her aloud, was burning a damned hole into my heart.

I didn't know if she could ever love me. The desire to make her understand was tortuous. Watching her pain was worse. I would take her burdens in a heartbeat, would that I could.

My jaw clenched so hard it hurt as her fingers brushed the stone covering my ribs.

The world needed us to win the Poseidon Trials. Aquarius and Olympus needed us to defeat Atlas. They needed us to find the Heart of the Ocean and rid the world of the stone blight.

But once Atlas and the blight were dealt with?

Then I would make things right.

I would tell Almi all the things I couldn't now. I could apologize and rid myself of the searing guilt that plagued me daily.

Almi would be happy.

My deal with Atlas had ensured that. She would live the life she had always wanted to live.

And it did not matter that she could not love me, because I would not be there to live it with her.

# ALMI

*W*hen we got close to the city I could see a pier jutting out of the dome, and Kalypso's ship was moored against it. Every building in sight either had sections missing, was crumbling to pieces, or was completely destroyed. It was a city of ruins, something I could imagine a human archaeologist would go nuts for.

*Mossy* pulled up alongside the pier, and I took a deep breath.

I had eaten as much as I could manage and put bread and dried meat in my magicked belt in case we needed more later. We had also drunk a vial each of Poseidon's energy stuff. Blue and Chrysos were on the bridge with us, stamping their feet and looking more ready to go than I felt.

This was the end. I knew it was, as surely as I knew I loved Lily.

We would either leave this place as victors, or we wouldn't leave at all.

The thought of spending eternity in the sunken, ruined city, as still and stone as everything else in it, made me want to keep my feet firmly on the planks of the deck.

But then Blue nudged me, and Kryvo spoke. "We will find all the shells." His quavering voice didn't hold a note of confidence, but the fact that he was trying to buoy me forced me into action.

"Of course we will, little friend. Of course we will."

I tried to lift myself onto Blue, and felt Poseidon's hands on my waist. Heat swooped through me as he lifted me easily onto the pegasus' back.

"Thanks."

He pulled himself onto Chrysos, and I caught his wince at the inflexibility of his side that was mostly covered in stone. "Are you ready?"

"As I'll ever be." Which was code for *I'll never be.*

The pegasi took off, the two of them bursting through the shield around the ship and swooping through the water to the dome. The distance was short enough that I didn't need the breathing bubbles, but my little whirlwind shot after us, whizzing around at my side.

I expected that we would need to find a point where water met the dome in order to get in, just like the domes in Aquarius, but Poseidon was ahead of me and he guided Chrysos straight at the silver barrier.

He and pegasus slipped straight through the dome, so I shrugged and followed him. Silence met us as we broke through the dome covering Atlantis.

As Blue descended, I got a better look at the buildings

around me. I could see that they would once have been grand, even the smaller ones. All pale, polished stone or marble, many of the surfaces were decorated with gilded patterns — or at least they had been once. The sound of the pegasi's hooves touching down on the flagstone ground echoed around us, and it wasn't until I twisted my body and slid off Blue's back that I saw the first statue.

I froze, my breath catching. It was a woman, her arm halfway up to shield her face, which wore an expression of true fear. Her other arm was extended by her side, holding back a boy of about ten. He was gazing in the same direction as the woman I assumed was his mother, but his expression was one of awe.

I stepped toward the stone figures. Guilt and pressure weighed down on me as a new thought occurred to me. What if the Heart of the Ocean could bring these people back from the stone? What if it wasn't just Aquarius who could be healed, but the ancient people of Atlantis too?

I felt something on my shoulder and whirled. "Don't dwell on them," Poseidon said, his voice heavy with sadness.

"Poseidon, do you think the Heart of the Ocean can cure these people too?"

"Cure? Almi…" He looked at me as though he wasn't sure what to say, his jaw tight. "Almi, the people who have been turned fully to stone… I do not know if they are alive inside there."

"You mean, if they're already stone they can't be cured?" Fear lanced through me, and a fresh wave of grief built inside me. "But Silos!"

"I do not know for certain," he said quickly. "But I do not think you should risk raising your hopes."

"You kept them all, though, in your palace, all the people turned to stone! You talked about saving them." I could hear the desperation in my voice.

"Of course I did. I couldn't give up any chance of hope. But I do not want you to think it is your fault if they cannot be saved."

I turned back to the stone woman. Could she be saved?

My eyes moved to her child. Would the lives of these strangers be worth the cost? Could I pay with my sister's life?

What if I did, and they stayed as they were now, cold and lifeless?

Before the overwhelming doubt could burrow its way in any further, Poseidon gripped my shoulder, spinning me back to face him.

"Focus on the task at hand. Find shells. Beat Atlas. You are under no pressure to decide anything now. Do you understand me?"

I stared into his face, feeling the weight lift slightly at his words.

Respite. I was finding respite in the form of deadly Trials and avoiding being turned into a monster, or stone. But honestly? *Anything* was preferable to deciding whether or not to end my sister's life.

We walked through the fallen city in silence, Blue and Chrysos staying close. There were stone people everywhere, some clearly aware of their impending fate, and some caught oblivious. My overactive imagination couldn't help but picture what it must have been like, Medusa stalking through the streets, turning everyone who looked at her to stone.

As we walked, I tried to make myself look at anything other than the people. The architecture was exactly what the human world thought of as ancient Greece. Temples with triangular roofs and tall columns, simple square buildings decorated with intricate carvings and paintings of landscapes, animals, and people. I didn't see a single building still standing as it would have been in its full glory, though it was easy to see how magnificent the city would once have been. Dark green moss grew across the pale ruins, and there was a dampness to the air that smelled of slightly sweet decay. When I looked up, rather than see the vivid blue ocean above me like in Aquarius, I just saw navy-hued darkness.

"Was Atlantis always underwater?" I asked Poseidon. I kept my voice hushed, as seemed to befit our environment.

"No. It was an island."

"Oh."

"I covered it with a silver dome when I sank it because I couldn't use a gold one. Gold is for Aquarius."

"Why create a dome at all?"

He glanced at me. "Medusa. She is not a being of the ocean."

The reminder that he had sent her to live alone down here for centuries made my skin crawl. "Did you ever consider that death might be kinder?"

There was a long silence before he answered. "Yes. Many times."

"Then…" I trailed off, unwilling to finish the question.

"Why didn't I kill her?" He finished for me. "I tried to. Twice."

My mind flashed on the passage I'd read I the book, about Poseidon making two trips to Atlantis with sick people, and returning with them healed.

"I read about you visiting Atlantis twice," I said slowly. "The author of the book believed you were taking sick people to the Font of Zoi."

"A ruse."

"What?"

"That was a ruse. Back then, the citizens of Olympus still had distant memories of the font so it was easy to play on their beliefs. I had no sick person with me, either time, though I let the world believe I had."

"You just came down here to kill Medusa?"

"Yes."

"And?"

"And I failed."

I looked around, uneasiness crawling all over me. Poseidon had failed to defeat her twice at full strength. And now we were in her territory, on her and Atlas' terms, and Poseidon was practically powerless.

I shuddered as I imagined her stepping out from behind every splintered column and shattered wall we passed.

"How did the city end up all destroyed?" I feared I already knew the answer.

"Most of the damage was done when it sank to the

bottom of the ocean. The damage in the west," he waved his hand to our left, "was done the last time I came here."

I swallowed. "Fighting Medusa?"

"Yes."

"Where is the Font of Zoi?" I asked, changing the subject. "In fact, what is a font?"

"It's just a fancy word for a fountain. There used to be a palace in the center of the city that housed it, but it was destroyed when Medusa was turned."

"Was the font not damaged?"

Poseidon glanced at me as we walked. "The Font of Zoi is more ancient than anything else in Olympus. It cannot be damaged."

"Oh. Good." I tried to ignore a family of stone statues on my right, standing crowed in a lopsided doorway. "Should we go there? To the old palace?"

Before Poseidon could answer me, Blue whinnied loudly ahead of us. He was in sight, and he was poking his large head into a crumbling doorway, stamping his feet.

We both broke into a jog to reach him. "What's up, Blue?"

The building he was interested in was remarkably intact, compared with a lot of the others around it. Walls stood only half crumbled between chipped columns, and when I looked up, I could see that a large part of the peaked roof was still there. It looked like it might once have been a temple. I peered through the precarious archway and saw that Blue was looking down at the marble tiles on the floor. Carved into the first one was the image of a shell.

"Look."

Poseidon moved behind me to look where I was pointing, his proximity making my skin tingle and my pulse quicken.

"I guess we've found our first test," he said grimly.

# ALMI

*T*he inside of the temple was gloomy, light only entering through cracks in the ceiling and illuminating a narrow corridor that served as the entrance. Trepidation filled me, knowing that anything could be lurking in the dark, waiting for us.

"Air?" My whirlwind sprang to life beside me, and I felt a little better.

"I shall enter first."

I opened my mouth to protest, but he had already stepped past me. I shook my head, and silently urged my whirlwind to move to his side.

Cautiously, we made our way into the ruins of the temple. As we walked down the dark hallway, I saw more shells carved on the large tiles beneath our feet. The marble would once have been shining and polished, but now dust covered everything. Poseidon paused in front of me, and I almost bumped into his back, I was concentrating so hard on the floor.

"What's wrong?"

"There is a new carving on the tiles." I stepped to his side and saw a carving of a snake on the central tile. The corridor was three tiles wide, and on the next row there was a carving of a tree on the left tile, nothing on the middle one, and a shark on the third. It was too dark to see what was carved into the tiles further on, but I could see faintly that there were images.

"Do you think it is some sort of puzzle?"

"I don't know." He twisted slightly and pulled a small throwing star from one of his leather straps. He tossed it onto the tiles before us. With a small clatter it landed on the shark. Nothing happened for a beat, then the tile flared with fire before disintegrating completely. Warm, flickering light came from the hole now in the corridor floor, and I gaped as I leaned forward, trying to see what was under there.

"Lava." Poseidon was taller than me and could see further.

"Shit. How do we know which tiles to step on?"

"I don't know."

"How many of those throwing stars do you have?"

"One more."

"Huh." I squinted down the corridor, totally unable to see where it ended. "I'm not sure that's going to get us very far."

"I think we should step on the tiles with no carvings." He sounded decisive.

I frowned at him. "Why?"

"Because I don't understand trees or snakes."

I blinked. "Do you understand sharks?"

"Yes."

"And the shark tile would have sent us to a fiery death."

He paused. "I see your point. But I still think we should jump over the first row, and land on the blank central tile."

I let out a sigh. I had no better ideas. "Throw your other star, to check it's safe."

He pulled the sharp little weapon from his strap, and carefully threw it onto the blank middle tile on the second row. The marble flared with fire, then melted away into dust, making the hole in the corridor floor twice as wide.

I put my hands on my hips. "That went well."

"At least we know which tile is safe in that row now," he said. "The tree tile."

I pointed down the indeterminably long corridor. "I have no idea how many of these we have to deal with, but I'm guessing quite a few."

"Then we had better get moving."

I sighed. The first row would be easy for Poseidon to get over, his legs were that much longer than mine. But I would have to jump. "'I'm going first," I said, keen to make sure my landing area was clear.

"Fine."

I held my breath and resisted the urge to close my eyes as I jumped over the first row, onto the tree tile. I saw a flare of light around my legs as I landed, felt heat, then the ground beneath me suddenly felt wrong. A scream gasped from my lips as the tile began to fall away from under me.

"Almi!" As Poseidon yelled my name I felt wind whipping around me, and then I was moving up instead of down. My whirlwind had expanded and wrapped around me, lifting me completely clear of the tile floor.

"Can you take me to the end of the corridor?" Adrenaline rushed through me as I whispered the question. The whirlwind whizzed a little faster, and then we were flying over the ground, zooming along the corridor.

I tried to take deep breaths as we raced along, a small opening letting in light coming into view at what I assumed was the end of the corridor. As we got closer, the opening got larger, until it became an arched doorway. Gently, my whirlwind set me down on my feet, right in the middle of the doorway. I gripped the stone frame of the arch as I stared into the room beyond.

"Almi! Almi, are you alright?" Poseidon's voice bellowed from the other end of the hallway.

"Yes!" I yelled back, unable to take my eyes from what I was seeing. "Can you bring Poseidon across the tiles?" I asked my whirlwind. With a little flurry that I took as a *yes*, it set off back up the corridor.

I heard a masculine cry, then a minute later the whirling current of air set the sea king down beside me. "Almi, I thought-" His words tailed off as he noticed what was in the room before us.

Treasure.

The room glowed gold, and not because of some magic ceiling or lighting device, but because it was filled from floor to ceiling with gold.

The whole space was set six feet below us, stone steps leading down to the room, which explained how it was so intact compared to the outside of the building. It looked like something a dragon should have been guarding, piles and piles of golden coins stacked everywhere, huge wooden chests standing open and brimming over with gems of every size and color imaginable.

"We have to find one tiny shell in all this," I breathed. "Where has it all come from?"

"Medusa must have been hoarding it. She's had many years to amass it all."

"You mean she's spent all these years combing through a dead city stealing everyone's valuables?" I stared at him.

He shrugged. "She had little else to do. And she is greedy and aroused by wealth and power."

I shook my head as I turned back to the room. Poseidon stepped onto the first stair, and I instinctively reached out and grabbed his shoulder. "Wait! What if it's like the Cave of Wonders, and if you touch anything but the shell, everything tries to kill you?"

He looked at me as though I'd hit my head. "What?"

"Don't touch anything except the shell," I said.

"How are we supposed to find the shell without touching anything?" He swung his arm out, gesturing at the ten-foot-high piles of treasure.

"I don't know," I scowled. "Just… be careful."

Together, we made our way down the stone steps, into the trove. The parts of the walls that I could see showed the Olympian gods on their thrones, regal and formal. Athena's owl perched on her shoulder, and part of Zeus was obscured by a colossal, gilded statue of what looked like an orchid. There was barely any floor space available to walk on, and I let out a low whistle as we passed a carved ship almost as big as I was, exquisite in its detail.

"We could be here for days."

"We do not have days."

"No shit." I looked at my whirlwind, now in little form and bouncing along beside me. "Do you know where the shell is?"

It zoomed around me head a couple times, then settled by my shoulder. "I'm taking that as a no. Kryvo? Any ideas?"

"No. Sorry. But I think you're right not to touch anything you don't need to."

"Kryvo says I'm right–"

Poseidon held up his hand. "Shh. Do you hear that?"

I fell silent, listening. After a second, I heard the slight clinking of metal. "Is that coins moving?" I whispered.

"I think so," he whispered back. As he turned in a slow circle, he pulled his blade from his one of his chest straps.

I mimicked him, drawing Galatea's dagger from my thigh. Fear trickled through me as my eyes darted between the piles of coins. My gaze froze as I spotted movement. A single coin, tumbling quietly down the side of one of the larger heaps of treasure.

"There!" I breathed, pointing. As Poseidon turned to the pile, it exploded. Coins, gems, goblets, and trinkets flew everywhere, showering the room as a massive snake erupted from where it had been hidden in the mountain of treasure. I barely had time to react as the reptile's enormous mouth snapped at Poseidon. He leapt backward, slashing his knife at the creature, as my whirlwind flew between them. It buffeted the snake's face, keeping it at bay long enough for me to take it in. It was as gold as the room we were in, gleaming with metallic scales, and it was so long I couldn't even see the end of its tail. It slithered away from the whirlwind, trying to move around behind us. I heard a loud crash, and when I looked in that direction, a slab of marble had descended over the doorway we had entered through. We were trapped.

Panic surged inside me, and I felt my connection to the whirlwind strengthen in response. "We need a way out!" I didn't know if I was telling Poseidon or my whirlwind, but both reacted. Poseidon jumped over the snake's body as it rounded him, moving in to snap its jaws at him again. Fangs glistened with saliva, and its head was as large as Poseidon's chest. He slashed fast with the knife, making contact just behind the snake's head. The creature hissed, retreating a little.

My whirlwind had abandoned the snake and was zooming up and down the walls, as though it was looking for something. I risked closing my eyes, so that I could try to concentrate on my magic.

It was looking for gusts of air or draughts, I realized as I let my senses merge with the air. It was looking for a way out, just as I had asked it to.

Something slammed into my legs, and my eyes flew open. Pain flared up from my shin, and I stumbled to the ground, the golden tail of the snake whipping past my face.

I tried to scrabble back to my feet, but I was too slow. The tail wound around my waist, yanking me up off the ground. Poseidon was still hacking at the snake's face as it lunged repeatedly for him, and I belatedly remembered Galatea's dagger in my hand. With a shout, I brought it stabbing down into the golden scales. When the blade first met them I thought it wouldn't pierce the shiny armor plating, but then the resistance vanished, and the steel sank into the snake's tail. It let out a hiss, then flicked me hurling from its grasp.

I couldn't help my shout of pain as I slammed into the solid stone wall. The air left my chest as I hit, then I crashed the few feet to the ground, landing awkwardly. Something cracked in my ankle, and pain so fierce it made me briefly dizzy washed through me. Fighting nausea, I tried to stand, failing on my first attempt. The pain in my leg was too much, and I sank back onto my butt.

"Almi!" Poseidon roared my name, but the snake wasn't letting up. The tail came powering back toward me.

I sent a silent plea to air, and my whirlwind charged into the fray, forcing the tail away from me before it got close.

A loud crack sounded behind me, and I leaned back, looking up at where the sound had come from.

There was a three-foot crack in the stone where I had hit the wall. As I watched, the crack grew. Slowly at first, then almost too fast to comprehend, it snaked its way up the wall, moving across the ceiling. The sound of stone breaking apart grew, and the snake paused. Casting its slitted reptilian eyes toward the ceiling, the snake gave a small quiver, then spun away from Poseidon, retreating into the mountain of coins and gold it had come from.

I tipped myself forward, onto my hands and knees. If I couldn't stand, then I would crawl. "Poseidon, I think we need to get out of here!" He was at my side in seconds, trying to pull me to my feet. My whirlwind was at my other side, trying to keep me upright. The cracking sounds had turned to crashing sounds. I threw a glance behind me just in time to see that the wall I'd hit was coming down. A mass of slabs and broken chunks of stone were tumbling toward us.

My whirlwind grew, spinning around us so fast that when the first few hunks of rock fell over our heads, they were blasted away. But the slabs were getting bigger, and there were too many of them for it to keep out. Especially with me weakening by the moment. My head was spinning, the pain in my leg drawing too much of my attention.

"The ceiling has come away on that side. We may be able to get out," Poseidon called, pointing up.

"How? If the whirlwind stops, we'll be crushed!" The stone debris built up around us in a ring, and if the whirlwind stopped shielding us for even a second, we'd be crushed by the collapsing building.

"Chrysos!" roared Poseidon. Gold wings flashed into view above us immediately. The pegasus swooped down, heedless of the falling rock, diving into the clearing the whirlwind created. There was nowhere near enough room for the horse to touch down, but Poseidon wound one arm tightly around my waist, and then jumped high as Chrysos reached us. To both my horror and astonishment, he caught onto the pegasus' neck, and the winged horse immediately began to beat her wings, lifting us out of the falling structure.

# ALMI

"*D*on't let go!" I shrieked, dangling from Poseidon's arm, and trying not to look at him dangling from Chrysos' neck. "He's super strong, he's super strong," I chanted, squeezing my eyes closed.

"I *am* super strong," Poseidon said, and I opened my eyes as Chrysos cleared the top of the building and soared the short distance back to the road. Poseidon landed lightly, tilting me gently to my feet. Chrysos' hooves clacked on the ground as she landed next to where Blue was anxiously chattering his teeth.

"Thanks, Chrysos," I panted. "I think my ankle is broken," I said, as I tried to put the tiniest bit of weight on it and searing pain met the movement. I stumbled, and Poseidon tightened his grip around me.

"We must rest."

"But we didn't get any shells." Guilt crashed through me, along with a surge of anger. We'd risked our frigging lives in that temple, and didn't even have a shell to show for it.

"Winning is not as important as living," he said seriously, looking at me. "Persephone's potion will heal your ankle quickly, but only with rest."

Another wave of dizziness and pain rocked me. "What if someone else finds the red shell and ends the Trial?"

"Then we leave this place without facing Medusa. That in itself will be a win."

"But your trident! Your realm." I stared at him.

"I'll win them back. Once I am healed."

I knew he didn't believe that. I could hear it in his voice, see it in his face. "Bullshit."

"Almi, I'm not arguing with you. If you want to force the truth from me, then fine. There is no way Atlas will allow this to end before we face his wife. This whole fucking sabotage of the Poseidon Trials is about his revenge with me."

I blinked, and let the words sink in.

He was right. Atlas was in charge. He was playing us, and everyone else.

"Fine. We'll rest."


Leaning on Poseidon's arm, I tried to hobble alongside him in search of a reasonably stable-looking place to rest. But I only got a few steps before being forced to take weight off my injured leg completely. I tried to hop, but Poseidon stopped moving, frowning down at me.

"You could give me a piggyback?" I said, trying to

make light of the fact that not being able to walk in a place as dangerous as this was a pretty big problem.

Poseidon narrowed his eyes, then in one swift movement bent down and scooped me up in his arms.

I suppressed a squeak, throwing my own arms around his neck in surprise. Tingles ran along me everywhere my skin pressed against his, and my breath came a little shorter. Avoiding my eyes, the sea god began to stride toward the building.

"Am I not heavy?" I asked awkwardly.

"My magic is weakened, not my body," he growled.

"Oh." He was seven feet tall and pure muscle. I probably weighed nothing to him. "Good to know."

He raised an eyebrow, finally flicking his eyes to mine. "That my body is in fine working condition?"

I gulped. "Yes."

"Have no doubt."

I didn't.

Half a mile later, he ducked cautiously under the crumbling doorway of the pale stone building, alert and tense as he looked around. Dusty light filtered in through cracks on the walls and ceiling, and as I looked around I saw that the place had once been someone's home. Mercifully, there were no statues inside. The room I had entered was one large living space, with a kitchen counter at the back, a long dining table in the middle and tall, expensive looking couches at the front. The soft furnishings had disintegrated to nothing, and I doubted the table-legs would hold if we put any weight on the tabletop. There was only one floor to the building, and three closed doors that I could see. Poseidon set me back on my feet gently.

"I'll check the other rooms," he said quietly. I nodded and steadied myself by gripping the arm of the couch behind me. To my surprise, it felt sturdy, if a little grimy.

Poseidon announced the building as clear a few minutes later. Some of my tension relaxing, I sank down onto my butt. Dust puffed up in a cloud around me, and Kryvo made an unhappy sound.

I coughed and Poseidon came over, waving the dust away with his hands. "I fear it will not be a comfortable rest. But I will secure the door, and at least it will be a safe one. Eat."

I did as I was told, undoing my belt and pulling things from the pouches. First, I drank the potion that Persephone had given us, and then I ate the meat-filled pastries we'd loaded up with from *Mossy's* galley.

When Poseidon returned from barricading the door with the top of the dining table, I passed him the remaining pastries. He lowered himself to sit beside me and ate.

"I have sent the pegasi back to the ship. I am not accustomed to nearly dying."

I wasn't immediately sure what to say. "I guess being immortal hasn't prepared you for that, huh?"

He had an intense look in his eyes as he stared at me. "No. It has not."

"How long have you been sick with the stone blight?"

"A while. But it has never felt like the encounters of the last few hours."

"You know, we nearly died quite a few times over the last week. You forgotten the corpse flower?" I shuddered just thinking about the toxic underwater plant.

"I was unconscious by the time I was almost dead," he said. "I was not staring down the jaws of death."

"What about when we nearly fell in the talontaur's mouth?" His mouth quirked at the corners, and I scowled. "How the hell is anything about that creature funny?"

"You do not like to be wrong."

"No. Does anyone?"

"Certainly not. But it is a particular trait of gods and royalty." His smile was spreading slowly, and my stomach squished. "You are more suited to the position of queen than you think you are, Almi."

I snorted, unable to hold his gaze. "Nonsense. I'm inexperienced, impulsive, and I usually have no idea what I'm doing."

"Yet you always find a way. You never give up. That is courageous."

"It's pigheaded stubbornness. Driven by my need to save Lily."

"You are good of heart. You help others when it has nothing to do with your sister. Like that boy in that town-"

He cut off sharply.

"Poseidon," I said slowly. "What boy in what town are you referring to?" My stomach was flipping as I spoke. I knew what boy he meant. But there was no possible way he could know about that.

The wild look filled his eyes, stormy and bright. "The boy you stole food for. The homeless boy."

When I had been in Germany, looking for the book, a boy of about eight, homeless and hungry, had begun hanging around my trailer. I had a pretty good routine of stealing bread and juice off the back of a delivery trolley that made its way around the neighborhood early, and I started taking a little bit extra to give to the boy. We spoke no words of shared language, but I had formed a bond with the kid. When I'd moved on, I'd worried about him a long time.

"How can you know about that?" I could feel energy rolling off the god, and I felt a little breathless.

"You were never alone, Almi," he said eventually.

"How do you know about the homeless kid?" I repeated.

"I watched you."

My mind blanked a moment, a million emotions rushing me. "You *watched* me?"

Poseidon held his hands up, speaking quickly. "Not permanently, or in a way that would take liberties. On my honor." He pressed a hand to his chest. "I would use my power to check in on you from time to time, nothing more."

I stared, still utterly confused. "Why? Why would you spy on me?"

"I was not spying on you. Although I appreciate it might feel like that. I was ensuring that you were safe."

"Protecting your asset?" I tried to struggle to my feet, needing space, needing to be further away from him. But my leg wouldn't allow it, and I fell hard onto my ass again.

Poseidon moved to help me, but I threw him a look that suggested if he came anywhere near me I'd kill him, and he stilled.

"Protecting my wife." His voice dropped low.

"Do you have any idea what it feels like to be told that a god has been secretly watching you your whole life?"

His jaw tightened. "I have been periodically making sure you were safe. That is all."

The implications of what he was saying sent thoughts barreling through my head. "You must have known I had the metafora compass. You must have known I was coming back to steal your ship."

He shook his head. "No. I stopped checking in on you over a year ago."

"Why?"

He took a long breath, his eyes loaded with unidentifiable emotion when he brought them back to my livid gaze. "It was too painful. I was falling in love with you."

My tumbling anger stumbled to a halt. I swallowed, staring. "How?" My word was a hoarse bark. "How can you fall in love with someone you don't know? Someone whose life you've ruined?"

"You fought back. You were always positive. You were everything I didn't have in my life. I found myself wanting you more and more." He held his hand up again. "I mean you, not your body. I never, ever watched you inappropriately. I wouldn't do that to anybody, least of all a woman I respect as much as you."

"I don't understand," I said on a breath, rubbing my hands over my face. Emotion overwhelmed me, disparate pieces of information ringing in my ears.

If I accepted that he was telling the truth and hadn't been perving on me in the shower for nearly a decade, then I found myself less angry with him. He had been looking out for me, which fit in with the man I was learning he was — one who did feel the consequences of his actions and wouldn't marry a girl and then dump her in a different world without another thought.

"I knew. The first day I met you and your sister."

"Knew what?" I was almost too scared to meet his eyes again.

"That it was you I was destined to fall in love with. Even then, with no power, you glowed like a fucking beacon to me. But I knew the rest of the prophecy. I knew that if we fell in love, you would die. But I also knew I needed the Heart of the Ocean. I had no choice. To save your life, I had to marry your sister.

When that went wrong, it was too dangerous to keep you anywhere near me, so I sent you to the human world. I naively thought you might feel less inadequate there than somewhere you were surrounded by people with power. I couldn't stay away, though. I watched you. And the more I saw of your spirit, I knew I had been right. I saw what I had done to you, separating you from Lily. I began to hate myself for it, but the more you hated me, the less likely I was to be the cause of your death. So I embraced it. I resigned myself to a life where my wife, the woman I desired more than life itself, had to hate me. I had to be the cause of your misery."

# ALMI

**M**y head was spinning by the time he stopped speaking. "I need you to leave." My voice was surprisingly calm.

His tight face darkened. "It is dangerous here. I can't leave you."

"Just go over there, to another room or something," I said, waving my hand a touch desperately, belying my level tone. "I need some space. Now."

Slowly, he stood up. With one last piercing look at me, he strode away.

When I heard the soft closing of a door, I tipped my head forward and let out a shuddering breath, silent tears flooding from my eyes.

My whole damned life had been a lie. I had spent years feeling so alone it hurt, and someone had been in love with me that whole time. Not just someone, my own fucking husband. The man I had been learning to hate more and more every minute I was away from my home and my sister.

But he'd done it all to try to save me. He had sacrificed his desire, made himself miserable, learned to hate himself as much as I had, to do what he thought he had to in order to keep me safe.

The pain in his face when he had spoken had been unbearable to watch. Was that why I had just sent him away?

I closed my eyes. *Lily?*

My mental voice was tiny when I said my sister's name.

There was no answer.

*Lily? Lily, I need you.*

Nothing.

"Poseidon!" I called his name, and the god ran back into the room, knife out and his body tense. He looked around for the threat, before his eyes landed on me. "She's not responding. Lily isn't responding."

He dropped to his knees before me, tucking his knife away. "Atlantis is probably blocking the mental communication," he said gently. Slowly, he reached his hand out, wiping a tear from my cheek with his rough thumb. A new one replaced it instantly.

"You think she's really talking to me? It's not me making her up?"

He nodded. "Yes."

"What if I can't talk to her because she's dead?" The words barely sounded as I said them, my voice breaking on the last one.

"She is not." His hand moved so that he was cupping the side of my face reassuringly.

"You don't know that! What if I used too much power,

and—"

His other hand moved, so that he was holding my jaw on both sides, forcing me to look directly at him. "Lily is safe. Atlantis is through a portal, and I am sure that is what is blocking her." He spoke slowly and firmly, and I found myself calming.

"Can you talk to you brother?"

"I do not want to risk using my power. But you are strong enough to try."

I blinked at him, then screwed my eyes shut. *Persephone? Can you hear me?*

There was no response. My heart rate slowed a little more.

"I don't think it's working," I told Poseidon. His grip on my face relaxed, and without thinking, my own hand shot up to stop his moving away.

He froze, staring at me. Waves crashed in his beautiful eyes. "I'm sorry," he said. "For everything I have done. And for telling you today. I should not have."

"You could have done it differently. You could have sent Lily with me."

"I wish I could. But she was sick, and I couldn't risk anyone else trying to get to her for the Heart of the Ocean. In my realm, I knew she was safe."

"You could have let me know I wasn't alone. You could have told me why I was sent away."

He nodded. "I believed you would just start again in the human realm, your memory of me angry and distant. I had no idea of the love between you and your sister. I am sorry. I got it so wrong."

For a second, he looked so human, so pained and

regretful. "You really did get it wrong." He cast his eyes down, unable to hold my tear-filled gaze. "But for the right reasons." His eyes darted back to mine, flaring with light.

"You will forgive me?"

"No. But I think I understand you."

He said nothing for a long moment, and being so close to him was becoming unbearable. The urge to move my lips to his was warring hard with the urge to slap him across the face. He had controlled my entire life, made every decision about my future for me without my knowledge, and then secretly watched me. And he had done everything he possibly could to put my life above his happiness.

"I will take understanding over forgiveness," he said eventually. Slowly, he stood up, running his fingers along my jaw as he did so, his reluctance to remove them from my skin almost tangible.

My hand flew up to stop his moving, but as I got within in an inch of touching him, I forced it back down.

This was dangerous territory. I could feel the charged emotion between us like I could feel my magic when I used it. It was real and powerful. And potentially lethal.

I hadn't known how I could love a man who had torn my family apart. But the god I'd learned to hate had been a lie.

Poseidon had been forced into so many situations he couldn't win, and he was painfully aware of the consequences of his actions.

He did not do anything lightly. He did not perform his tasks with his own satisfaction as his motivation. And what he had done to me and Lily was just the same. Selfishness had not driven his choices. There hadn't been a right course of action that he'd willfully ignored.

I didn't love him. But I no longer believed that I couldn't.

And as I stared into his eyes, I knew Lily and Persephone had been right.

He loved me.

# ALMI

"*I* think I will give you that space," he said, voice husky.

I nodded. "Yes. But, Poseidon?"

His unearthly blue eyes bore into mine. "Yes?"

"Come back. I don't want to sleep alone."

"Anything, for my Queen."

He turned, striding away from me, toward one of the doors. I slumped, leaning my back against the couch and rubbing my hands over my face. What a mess. What a disastrous fucking mess.

"He is an extraordinarily complicated man." Kryvo's squeaky voice was thoughtful.

"That's an understatement," I muttered, instantly feeling a little less alone for hearing the starfish.

"But I suppose that you are fairly complicated too."

"Really? I'm simple."

"Your goals are simple. But your situation is not."

I rubbed my thumbs across my temples. "It's more

simple than it seems. Poseidon and all of Aquarius, or Lily."

"That's if you survive long enough to need to make that decision."

"Thanks for the reminder."

"Almi, you need some sort of blindfold for when you are back out there. Looking into Medusa's eyes will end all of this instantly."

I nodded, the practical advice what I needed to help drag me from my emotional rollercoaster.

Poseidon was in love with me. I needed to accept that, appreciate the danger that carried, and move on. The more I dwelled on what he had done for me, or at least, what he had tried to do for me, the more I risked my own feelings deepening. And if I died I wouldn't be able to save him or Lily.

"Yes. Very good idea, Kryvo." I gathered up as much control over my thoughts as I could, trying to focus on anything that wasn't the sea god or my sister. "Can you tell me another story from your murals?"

"Of course. What kind of story would you like?"

"Nothing romantic. Got anything heroic? A comeback from unlikely odds tale?"

"I have just the thing."


As Kryvo told me stories from the paintings in the palace, I collected stale-smelling cushions from the couches and made an uncomfortable bed on the floor. The throbbing in my ankle had lessened considerably, and I let the little starfish lull me to sleep, focusing enough on his words and the escapism of his stories to block out my own tumbling thoughts. I woke briefly when Poseidon joined me, his massive presence a comfort. He stayed a foot away from me, and I suppressed my groggy desire to tuck myself against his body. I had first hand experience of how he could make me feel, so I knew for sure that intimacy could literally kill me.

That didn't stop me dreaming about him the second I slipped back into sleep though.

It was a good thing that Poseidon was no longer next to me when I woke the next day. Desire was pounding through me, the tingling memories of my dream impossible to shift.

"Snap out of it, Almi," I muttered as I sat up, looking around for the god. "He spied on you for almost a decade. He's an asshole."

Except, he wasn't. And I knew it. I'd known it since he'd saved me from the rotblood when I'd tried to reach his palace. That day seemed like a lifetime ago.

"How is your ankle?" His voice startled me, and I swiveled on my butt to see him coming in through the no-longer barricaded door.

Carefully, I stood, testing my leg.

I couldn't believe that I had been completely unable to put weight on the same foot just the day before. The injury was healed. I lifted my uninjured leg, putting all of my weight on the bad ankle. It was fine, no trace of any damage left, no pain or discomfort. Not even a twinge.

"If you're watching, Persephone, you're my hero," I said, speaking to the gloomy room in general.

I packed up the things I'd taken out of my belt, munching on a hunk of dried meat as I did.

"Kryvo suggested I make some sort of blindfold," I told Poseidon when he asked me if Iw as ready to leave. He was being overly formal and I knew he was as concerned about our precarious emotional connection as I was.

"Excellent idea." He gripped on of the leather straps across his chest and it glowed briefly blue.

"You shouldn't be using any magic!"

He shook his head at my protest. "It's not my magic. It's the toga's magic." Slowly, he drew his fingers away from the light, the watery material of his toga appearing between his fingertips, expanding fast.

"That's awesome."

He raised an eyebrow, then fished his knife from another strap. Carefully, he cut a slice of fabric from the bottom of the toga. I watched with a twinge of regret.

"I'm not surprised your ship doesn't like me. I bet your toga isn't much of a fan either."

"Both can be repaired," he said, straightening and handing me the strip of aqua-green fabric. Tiny little white tipped waves rolled across it, and I felt inexplicably attached to it. "You, on the other hand, can not be repaired, if you are turned to stone. Be careful, Almi."

I broke his intense gaze and nodded. "Always. Let's go."

Blue and Chrysos were outside in the street when we left our temporary shelter, and Blue trotted to me as soon as he saw me.

"Morning, gorgeous," I said to the pegasus as he

nudged my hands hard with his snout. "You sleep okay?" He whinnied at me, flicking his tail uneasily. I couldn't blame him for his anxiety. There was something unnerving about the streets of the silent sunken city of Atlantis, even without the constant worry of Medusa lurking about. The light in the whole place was wrong, the only illumination coming from the icy silver dome over our heads. Beyond that the darkness was suffocating, and if I looked up too long I felt the panic starting to build inside me.

"We must go to the palace." I looked at Poseidon in surprise. "I thought you said that's where they will expect you to go?"

"It is. I am tired of these games. I want this done." What he wasn't saying aloud was that he was weakening with every passing day. I could feel the energy coming from him depleting, his powerful aura less each day.

"I'm right there with you," I said with a nod. "Let's get this over with."

# ALMI

*W*e walked for what I thought was about an hour, Poseidon confident in the direction. Eventually we rounded a corner and the monotony of grey stone was finally interrupted. And not by anything I would have expected.

Green moss had grown all over all the fallen stone, and ivy was crawling up the columns that still stood, along with some of the statues.

Thirty feet away, blocking the road we were walking down, was a ten foot tall hedge. Perfectly trimmed into a large rectangle, and vivid green against the cool grey and pale blue of the rest of our surroundings, it looked anything but innocent. There was a small gap carved into the middle of it. An entrance.

"I think we're about to enter a maze."

Poseidon looked at me. "You mean a labyrinth?"

I nodded. "What is the difference?"

"A labyrinth is filled with things ready to kill you."

"Then yeah, I guess we're about to enter a labyrinth." I

thought about what I knew about mazes, or labyrinths. You had to get to the middle. Mild claustrophobia simmered when I thought about being trapped or lost in an endless deadly maze. "Can't we just ride Blue and Chrysos to the middle?" I suggested hopefully.

Poseidon looked at the pegasi, stopped still next to us. Chrysos flexed her stunning golden wings , as if to say she was up for it.

As Poseidon opened his mouth to answer though, a loud buzzing started up.

"What's that?" My whirlwind sprang to life beside me, and Poseidon has his blade drawn. The sound was coming from above us though.

A swarm of something dropped through the air above us, separating as they got closer. They were small and gleaming gold, and I thought they looked a lot like bees. No, hornets. Huge stingers on their butts angled toward us as Poseidon and I slashed with our daggers, trying to keep them back. My whirlwind zoomed about, blasting them away. One of the pegasi made an awful shrieking whinny.

"Blue!" The pegasus had launched himself into the air in a frenzy, his wings beating at the swarm of creatures around him, his mouth frothing as he snapped his jaws at them. But they were relentless. The swarm had abandoned me and Poseidon, instead splitting themselves between the two winged horses. Chrysos was stamping and jumping, trying to keep her wings tucked in, but I could see the creatures landing on her broad flanks, their stingers piercing the hide.

Blue made another awful sound, and fear and anger

had me surging toward them. My whirlwind was trying to bat them back, but there were so many, and it could only help one pegasus at a time.

"Go back tot he ship!" shouted Poseidon. Blue's eyes found mien, as though he wanted my permission to leave.

"Go!"

Chrysos launched into the air, and with one last frantic look, Blue soared off through the sky, leaving most of the swarm unable to keep up.

My whirlwind shot back to my side, ready to defend me fro the remaining golden insects, but with another loud buzz, they flew off, melting into the hedge before us.

I stood panting slightly, furious that Blue had been attacked. "Do you think they were sent just to stop us flying?"

"Yes." Poseidon looked as furious as I felt.

"Fuckers."

He nodded. "They will pay."

"Fucking right, they will." The angry adrenaline had been just what I needed to shift my trepidation. "They'll pay now. Let's go." Without giving myself time to panic, I strode into the labyrinth, Poseidon right by my side.

The hedges rose up high on either side of us, dense enough that I couldn't see through them, and tall enough that we wouldn't be able to climb over them. The air had cooled, and the pine scent held a tinge of sweet rot. Silence swallowed us as we walked, so complete it was as unnerving as the solid walls of green surrounding us.

The path was straight, and it was a few moments before we reached a fork. "Left or right?" I whispered.

"If we always turn the same way, we should find the center."

"Okay. Let's go left."

Poseidon turned, and we carried on, daggers drawn. There was the distinct feeling of being watched, and it made my skin crawl. The more corners we turned, the more I became convinced there would be something waiting for us round each one. Someone waiting for us. Medusa.

Poseidon paused before me, and my heart skipped a beat, pumped up as I was. "What's wrong?"

"There's something ahead." I squinted. I could make out something grey along the long straight path in front of us.

"Shall we go back? Or try to find a turning?" There were no gaps in the hedge on our left, but I could see one further down on the right. But that would ruin our plan of always turning left.

"Let's see what it is," he murmured.

I nodded, my whirlwind expanding slightly beside me in response to my building fear.

It was a statue. We didn't need to go much further before the stone structure became clear. It was in the middle of the path, about as large as Poseidon, and it was of a cyclops. Even form a distance I could see how detailed its features were, and I wondered if it had once lived, or if it was a product of the imagination of a talented sculptor.

"The hedges," whispered Poseidon. I looked left and

right, and started in surprise. Stone faces filled the gaps between the tick foliage.

"That's why I feel like I'm being watched," I hissed. "Jeez. They're creepy as hell."

"I think we should go past the cyclops."

"I agree." We had stuck to the left-turning plan so far, and I had no intention of undoing our progress and getting lost.

Slowly, we inched our way toward the imposing statue. I knew it was made form stone, but that didn't stop my nerves as we reached it. The monsters face was a mask of anger, his fists the size of my head.

A tiny cracking sound reached my ear as Poseidon squeezed past the statue, trying not to touch the hedge.

"What was that?"

"Just keep moving," he said, voice tight.

I did as he said, slipping more easily past the cyclops on the other side. Another cracking sound pierced the eery silence. I looked back at the statue. It looked solid, and I could see no movement.

I looked ahead again, seeing a turning on out left in a few feet. "There," I pointed, and together we picked up our pace.

The path that came into view when we turned was peppered with statues and I faltered. A flash of gold caught my eye at ground level.

"Snake."

Tiny golden snakes were slithering across the path between the statues. I watched as one wound its way around the closest one, a small satyr with evil looking eyes.

"I don't like this."

"If it is getting more dangerous, then we are on the right path," Poseidon replied grimly.

"Small comfort."

We moved forward, my every sense on high alert. Tiny hissing sounds perforated the heavy silence, making me even more on edge.

The satyr blinked.

A yelp of shock left me, and it was as though the sound brought everything around us to life. About half the statues moved, the satyr springing forward. For a thing made of stone, he moved effortlessly. A roar behind him drew my attention, and I saw a stone griffin swiping at another statue that appeared to be inanimate.

My whirlwind danced forward, catching the satyrs heavy arm as it started to swing. Poseidon ran beyond it, launching his dagger at the griffin.

In the water, my air had removed my enemies by blasting them away, and I compelled my whirlwind to do exactly that. But these were no ordinary stone beasts. The resistance I felt when the whirlwind tried to heave the satyr off the ground was massive.

"You lifted Charybdis, you can do this!" But I felt myself exhausting fast, and knew this stone was magicked with something strong. Titan magic.

"Run! Our best bet is to run past them!" Poseidon called from ahead of me. Taking a deep breath, I did as he said, and sprinted past the satyr.

My whirlwind followed me immediately, and as I caught up with Poseidon, who was sparring with the mean-looking griffin, he tucked in his knife arm and began to run with me. We ducked and dived the swiping, lumbering statues as we sprinted, leaping over golden snakes that I was sure were increasing in size.

We almost missed a left turn, but I skidded to a stop as I just caught it in my peripheral vision. "Here!"

We barreled around the corner and saw a mercifully empty path ahead. "Are they following?" We both turned, my whirlwind bouncing, ready. But there was nothing behind us, and silence had settled once more.

I leaned over, gripping my knees as I tried to get my breath back. I was not much fitter than I'd been when I'd last sprinted that fast, away from a stacked librarian when I'd stolen the book. I shook my head as I straightened. So much had changed since then.

"Are you alright?"

"Yes. Running isn't my thing."

"We should keep moving." A snake slithered across the path before us, making me jerk up straight. It was three of four times the size of the first one I had seen, thick and long and shining with gold scales as it moved between the hedges.

"Agreed."

We resumed walking, and I tried to ignore the continued stone faces in the hedges. Most were humanoid, and all had detailed eyes that followed us as we kept turning left. A steady stream of snakes crossed our path, and with each one I knew we were getting closer to an attack of some sort. It made no sense to me that they were ignoring us. Not when there were so many, easily enough to be a threat.

After what felt like another hour, but was probably

less, I heard a low loud slithering sound. Poseidon slowed at the same time I did. The noise of twigs snapping and foliage scraping increased.

"Are you thinking what I'm thinking?" I whispered, pulse racing.

"Our golden friend from yesterday," Poseidon growled.

I tensed, my whirlwind growing again. "I owe him one. He fucked my leg up." My bravado was only partially real. The giant snake scared the shit out of me. Not as much as the idea of wandering the cursed maze for the rest of time, but plenty enough to make my knees feel funny.

Sure enough, seconds later, a massive golden snake head appeared around the corner ahead of us. It's huge forked tongue flicked out at us, hovering and tasting the air as we froze. Its powerful body, filling the entire pathway and scraping on the hedges as it moved, slithered into view behind the head.

"What's our plan?" I hissed, trying not to sound frantic and failing.

"Snakes have a weak point at the back of their skulls. You distract it, I'll stab it."

Before I could say a word in reply, Poseidon roared, and ran at the snake.

"Go!" I threw my arm forward, and my whirlwind rushed after him.


The snake had little time to react before Poseidon reached it. He threw himself low to the ground, skidding under its raised head, then grabbing onto its neck. His arms could barely close around it, it was so large, but he swung himself up and onto the things back.

The snakes thrashed and hissed, its tail flicking up behind him and powering down, toward Poseidon. My whirlwind got there first though, slamming into the oncoming tail that had made such easy work of me the day before. As if getting revenge for me, the whirlwind hammered angrily at the snake's tail, hindering any chance it had at all of reaching Poseidon.

The creature was thrashing its head so hard Poseidon could keep any kind of purchase on it. Its jaws were wide open, fangs bared. It could probably have swallowed me whole. But Poseidon wasn't going to be able to defeat it on its own. Gathering my courage, I ran forward.

Throwing my arms in the air, I yelled at the snake. "You broke my ankle, you big ugly brute!"

The snake paused for the briefest second as it it saw me jumping up and down in front of it. A second was all Poseidon needed. I watched as he raised his blade with both hands and expertly brought it plunging down, right behind the monsters head. I saw the things eye's flash with surprise, then flare red before it collapsed to the ground.

Poseidon's gaze locked on mine, and he tugged his dagger free, leaping off the snake's back.

An hissing wail echoed through the air, angry and chilling.

"I think we just killed Medusa's guard dog," said Poseidon.

I swallowed, looking at the dead snake. "That was impressive," I murmured.

"It's one more reason for her to hate me. We are close."

"To the center of the maze?"

"To the Font of Zoi. I can feel it. You should be able to too."

I concentrated on the air, trying to feel for magic. A thrumming was coming from our left. A lively, dangerous sort of thrumming.

Together, we left the golden snake on the ground, and headed for the font.

# ALMI

*P*oseidon hadn't been kidding when he'd said a font was just a fancy name for a fountain. And it wasn't even a fancy-looking fountain. I could see a simple stone pedestal in the center of the maze, the stone the same gray color as the stone that covered Poseidon's skin. There was a bowl on top of the pedestal, smooth and a shade paler, and water gently bubbled up in the middle of it, only rising a few inches off the surface before splashing back down.

For all its simple appearance, nobody would have believed the font to be harmless. It oozed power, the air around us thick with thrumming energy. It only added to my tension as I looked around cautiously.

The space seemed to be clear of anything living, only the foreboding green of the hedges surrounding us.

Something flashed red above the font, and my focus zoned in on it. A red shell, flitting around a few feet above the bubbling water.

"Look!" I moved to step closer, but Poseidon gripped my arm.

"It is too easy. Something is wrong." His voice was a hiss, and fresh trepidation took me.

Movement caught my eye and I saw a golden snake slither into the clearing on the other side. It sped toward the font, then began to twine its way around the base. A second later another snake followed, then another.

A low, booming laugh began to sound, almost too low to make out at first, then gaining in volume.

"I can't tell you how much I wished that you had gotten here first, Poseidon." Atlas voice echoed around us. "My wife has been expecting you, but she found poor old Polybotes instead."

The air behind the font shimmered, and a ten foot tall statue appeared.

Polybotes.

His face was a mask of anger, his hands half raised to cover his eyes.

My stomach was knotting itself in fear, anticipation making me feel sick as whirlwind grew beside me.

"You are not supposed to interfere with the Trial! You gave Athena your word," shouted Poseidon, anger hard on his face as he stared at the stone giant.

"You were not supposed to do a great many things, sea king," Atlas snarled. With a flash of red light he appeared in the clearing, in front of the font. "I destroyed the palace that used to house this font after my wife told me what you tried to make her do in there." Every word was dripping with hateful venom, and flames licked over his armor. "And now its new home is where you shall watch your own wife meet the same fate."

"Your wife lied to you." I said the words loudly, and both men turned to look at me.

"Is that what he told you?" Atlas spat.

"Yes. And I believe him."

"Of course you do. It does not make it true."

"Have you asked her?"

"I will not insult her honor by doing any such thing!" he roared, and his manic rage instantly made me understand why Poseidon had not bothered to try to defend himself with the truth. Atlas would clearly have it no other way, there would be no convincing him that his wife had been in the wrong or lied to him.

Kryvo's tiny, urgent voice came to me. "Almi, she is coming. I can feel her magic, you need to shield your eyes, now."

I pulled out the strip of fabric from Poseidon's toga that he had cut me, and quickly tied it around my head, flush over eyes.

The darkness swallowed me and I felt desperately helpless as Atlas began to laugh.

"That will not save you, silly little Queen."

Panic that had started as a creeping feeling began to wash over me in waves as I heard slithering noises around me, followed by the movement of my whirlwind.

"Poseidon?" I tried to keep my voice quiet and free of alarm, but I knew I had failed.

"I am here," he answered just as quietly.

"This isn't going to work. I can't see. I can't fight or control my air if I can't see."

Atlas' laughter was getting louder, and so was the slithering sound.

My little starfish spoke, his voice barely audible over both sounds. "I have found a starfish! I can show you what is happening through their eyes!"

"What? How have you found-" I started to say, but then my words failed me as a vision descended over the blackness.

I was looking at the scene from the center of the courtyard, and I realized dimly that the starfish Kryvo had found and was using to show me the view must have been on the font itself. I could see myself standing next to Poseidon, my whirlwind high and fast next to me, and Poseidon's blade drawn. I could hardly see Atlas as he was standing next to the font, only his side making into my fixed view.

None of that seemed important though, compared with what was moving into the clearing with us.

There were so many golden snakes slithering across the ground and around the bottom of the font now that almost the whole ground was covered, and they parted like water for the bare green feet gliding through them.

Medusa.

She was exactly as Poseidon's painting had depicted. Beautiful and terrifying. An ivory white toga covered most of her scaled green skin, and the snakes making up her hair were as bright as Atlas' golden armor. Her piercing eyes were fixed on me, and I shuddered. I knew for certain that if it weren't for the blindfold, I'd be stone already.

"Poseidon. Long time no see."

Her voice was a hiss that made my skin crawl, and I sucked in a breath as fear made my heart beat even faster.

"This is your last chance to tell your husband the truth," Poseidon said.

She laughed, soft and even more hiss-like. "My last chance? We have faced each other before and you have never offered such ultimatums." She paused, tilting her head. All the golden snakes rose together. "Ah, but you are as good as dead already, you poor immortal." She tipped her head back and laughed again, loudly this time. The sound made me feel sick.

"Husband dear, I told you I infected him last time."

"You were right, my darling. And now these little friends have infected his whole realm, and soon all of Olympus."

"No. This ends today."

"Wrong," said Atlas. "The only thing that can cure the stone blight is the Heart of the Ocean. And I shall soon be in possession of that."

"How?" The single word escaped my lips.

Medusa's hiss answered me. "Why are you wearing that ugly blindfold, little queen? Show me your beauty and take it off," she said, sickly sweet. My whirlwind sped up, whipping a path in front of me, then back again, like a guard dog might to warn off a threat. The disorientation of watching myself from the font made me feel off balance as I pulled Galatea's dagger from my thigh.

"The heart of a Nereid," Atlas said, stepping closer to me and Poseidon and putting his back into my line of sight. I watched his shoulders shrug. "Poseidon interpreted the Oracle's prophecy differently than I did. He took the term possession to mean ownership by marriage. But I took the liberty of checking in at Delphi myself, and can confirm that cutting the heart from the chest, locking it in a box and declaring it as my own will work just as efficiently."

Poseidon's face turned so dark with anger, if he'd had his full power I would have run away from him myself. "You will not touch her."

"I have two to choose from," Atlas said, and snapped his fingers.

Lily appeared in the middle of the clearing.

My heart skipped a beat as everything around me stilled, shock taking over my senses.

She was asleep, barely any patches of skin on her exposed face and arms not covered in stone. The golden snakes began to slither over her body and impulse took over.

"Get off her!" I began to move forward, kicking at the snakes. Medusa opened her mouth, a hideous hiss issuing from it, and Poseidon's hand shot out, yanking me back by the shoulder.

"You can not harm her!" Poseidon shouted.

"Yes, yes, yes, I remember our deal." Atlas waved his hand dismissively. "This sleeping sister is only my back up, in case my wife accidentally kills yours. I am very keen that little Almi here is the one who's heart I cut out and keep. I am hopeful that whatever creature the font turns her into doesn't need her heart to keep her alive." I couldn't see Atlas' face but his voice sounded as crazy as I had ever heard it.

I tried to work his words out, tried to think of

anything I could do. "What deal is he talking about?" I said, turning my blind head to Poseidon. "Why is Lily here? I thought you said she was safe in the palace!" The view I had from the font didn't change, and frustration churned up with my fear, making my pulse race so fast my hands began to shake.

"Enough!" Atlas clapped his hands again, before Poseidon could say anything. "Say goodbye to your husband, Almi. I was never afforded the opportunity to do so with my wife, before Poseidon turned her into what you see now."

"I have come to terms with this body, husband dear," Medusa hissed. "I have not however, come to terms with being sent to live for centuries alone at the bottom of the godforsaken ocean."

For an instant, I saw regret on Poseidon's face. Then Medusa attacked.

# ALMI

*M*y whirlwind sprang to my defense, and gratitude for the fact that I could see through the starfish statue flooded me as I directed it toward the shrieking snake-woman.

The need to defend not just myself but my unconscious sister and the powerless Poseidon was booming in my mind, and the whirlwind smashed into Medusa before she could get close to me, her clawed hands raised and ready.

Atlas roared and hurled fire toward me. Before I could react, a wall of water erupted from Poseidon, shielding us both from the fire and instantly dousing it. Medusa barreled forward again, trying to force her way through my whirlwind, which was buffeting her this way and that.

Atlas hurled more fire at us, and fear for Poseidon flooded me. He couldn't keep using his power without turning to stone. But I couldn't fight Atlas *and* Medusa with my air, I needed his help. I didn't know how to split the whirlwind, didn't have the strength or power to control two separate forces. Frustration and fear were building up in my gut, adrenaline only fueling them.

"You can't kill me, and you know it!" shouted Poseidon.

Atlas' response was loud, madness lacing his words. "I don't want to kill you, sea king. I want to maim you. I want to hurt you. I want to immobilize you, so that you can do nothing but bleed and weep, while the woman you loves is turned into a monster."

An explosion of hatred poured through me, the idea of Poseidon hurt intolerable. My sister's unconscious form on the ground before me, her body being used as bait in this fucked-up bid for revenge against a man I had come to realize would do no harm to an innocent, was suddenly too much.

The roiling emotions hardened inside me, forming a giant ball of pure rage. The whirlwind split in two.

I stared, shocked for a second, then pressure crushed in on my head as the power of the two separate columns of wind churned around in me. I directed one to keep Medusa away from Poseidon, and as I tried to compel the other one toward Atlas, I saw the dark form of Kalypso running into the clearing. I watched her eyes flick over the scene, and her shudder as she saw Medusa. When her gaze fell on the font, her dark eyes sparkled.

"Yes, my daughter!" roared Atlas. "Take the red shell! You and Ceto are even, if you take it now, you will win!"

Daughter? Well that fucking explained a lot.

Throwing her arm up across her eyes, Kalypso ran toward the font.

I compelled one of the whirlwinds toward her, trying to stop her reaching the font. But her outstretched arm was too close, and the implications of what she was about to do roared through my head.

She would win. She would win the Trident, Aquarius, and control of Poseidon's life. And she would let Atlas tear it apart. The snakes would fill Aquarius, turning everyone to stone, completing the Titan's revenge. And then? Atlas' maniacal cackle echoed through the clearing as she got close.

And then he would challenge the whole of Olympus. I was certain.

I knew what I had to do. Crushing sadness weighed down on me, so hard it made my vision blur.

But the decision had been made.

It had been made for me.

It was simply impossible to trade the lives of hundreds for one.

A sob tore from my throat, and a sharp feeling hit me in the chest. For a split second, I thought some sort of dart had been thrown at me, then I felt the rage no longer pouring through me, but *from* me.

My whirlwinds shuddered a second, then grew, pulsing with bright silver light. In my chest, the feeling was turning from painful to downright explosive.

My head swam as power coursed from my body, out into the mass of air before me. Golden snakes were picked up from where they were trying to escape and hurled through the air.

My head swam with the rush of power, and somewhere deep inside, fear crawled up through me.

Power.

*So much power.*

I hurled both whirlwinds at Kalypso, just as her hand was inches from the red shell.

She screamed as she flew thirty feet in the air. Atlas gaped, and with a sickening satisfaction, I launched the goddess as far away from the font as I could manage.

I reached up, desperate to tear the blindfold from my eyes. I needed to see my tattoo.

I needed to know for sure if I really had just embraced my power.

*If I had killed my sister.*

"Almi, no!" Poseidon's voice wasn't just insistent, it held actual power, and my hand halted where it was.

With one tiny thought, I threw his magic from me, lifting my hand the rest of the way.

"Almi, she'll kill you! She'll kill you instantly!" Kryvo's voice was shrill, but my fingers tugged the blindfold away, regardless.

I had my head angled down, and the vision from the font faded, my own eyes stinging and blurry in the light as my chest came into view.

My tattoo.

It was beautiful. As bright and as vivid as Lily's had ever been.

I'd have given anything in the world at that moment to rid every speck of color from my skin.

"I'm sorry!" My words were a sob, and I screwed my eyes closed and dropped to my knees.

When I was sure I was looking at the floor, I opened them again, crawling through the mass of snakes toward my sister. They hissed and bit at me, hundreds of lacerations covering my skin as I powered through them. I didn't care.

"Keep her away!" I screamed at air. Anger and resentment laced my words, but so did unbridled power. I was a ticking fucking time-bomb, so loaded with power it was making my head swim and everything blur. The fact that I hadn't been yanked off my knees by Medusa suggested that air was doing as I had commanded.

I reached Lily, pulling her head onto my lap. Tears were streaming down my face so thick and fast I couldn't see properly. For a second, I thought her eyes moved.

I shouted again, the noise animal and strangled and pure grief.

Lily's eyes flickered open.

"Lily?" I was crying so hard the word barely sounded.

"Almi," my sister croaked.

"Lily!" I pulled her too me, trying to hug her mostly stone body, my heart smashing so hard against my ribs. "Lily, you're awake! You're alive!"

I moved so that her head was in my lap again, and I could look into her face. She beamed at me. "I'm so proud of you."

"What's happening?"

"A few things, I think," she smiled. "First, I am awake because your grief caused Poseidon enough pain that he wept a tear for you. Gods don't cry, Almi."

I started at her, the words of the prophecy ringing in

my ears. She will sleep until the gods weep. All this time, making Poseidon cry would have woken her?

"What about my power?"

Her smile softened. "Don't blame yourself, Almi. It was always going to happen like this. You made the right decision. I'm just so pleased I got to say goodbye."

"No, no, you're awake now! It's going to be okay!"

"Listen to me, Almi. There's not much time. Poseidon made a deal after he flashed you out of the bakery. My life, for his."

"What?"

"The only way he could stop Atlas from cutting out my heart was to offer up his own life. Poseidon agreed that if I was still alive and safe at the end of the Trials then Atlas could have his life, to do with as he wished. But if I died, then Atlas had to remove his trident as a prize in the Trials, and give it back to Poseidon."

"But…"

"I know it wasn't the plan, but by embracing your power, you've broken that deal."

My mouth opened and closed as I tried to make sense of what she was saying. Only one thing was repeating. "You're dying."

"Yes. I've been dying for a decade, Almi. It's time. And like I said before, how lucky am I to have helped my little sister save the world?" Her smile was sad and soft, and fresh grief crashed through me.

"Please. Please stay with me."

"I've stayed as long as I can. You have someone else to love now."

"No." I shook my head, eyes blurred with tears.

"I love you, Almi."

"I love you," I sobbed back.

I knew when it happened, just a second later. I felt the life leave her. And with it went all rational thought.

The time-bomb exploded.

# ALMI

*W*hen I looked up, it wasn't with the thought of avoiding Medusa's stare. It was with the thought of annihilating her completely.

A sense of utter invincibility had taken me, and somehow, somewhere, I knew I had changed. Poseidon said he was immune to her gaze because he was a god. Well, the power roaring through my veins now had to equal that of a fucking god, and I was going to use it.

I didn't speak a word of command as I rose to my feet, but air whooshed to me instantly. It whirled around me, creating a barrier like the one it did when I was underwater. With no fear inside me at all, I took in the scene before me.

While I had been with Lily, Ceto had reached the clearing. And to my relief, she was fighting alongside us. Snakes poured from Medusa's outstretched claws, and they covered the sea monster's body. Inky red liquid burst from the spots all over her tentacles as Ceto blasted the snakes back at Medusa.

Poseidon was facing Atlas, my silver-glowing whirlwind beating against the fire god every time a flame even tried to leave his fingertips.

As I started to move toward them, gold light beamed from Poseidon's hands, and I heard him cry out in surprise. Both he and Atlas froze as the light flared too bright to look at, then died away. There, gleaming in Poseidon's open hands, was his golden trident.

Atlas turned to look at me, then down at Lily, his face an angry snarl. Poseidon looked at me too and his expression made my shattered heart skip a beat. There was no triumph in the return of his precious trident. Only pure sorrow. Lily's words spoke loudly in my mind.

I'd been so overwhelmed with grief, so astonished to hear her actual voice, the impact of what he'd done had been lost.

But now, staring at him, seeing my own pain echoed in his fierce eyes, it hit me.

He had traded his life for hers.

He was willing to die, to save my sister. For me.

Searing pain lanced through my gut, and I gasped as it reached my chest, a crushing agony gripping me, forcing me to my knees once more.

Atlas' snarl turned into a delighted grin as Poseidon shouted my name. He began to run toward me, but there was a shriek from Ceto, and then Poseidon's legs were suddenly stone. He beat at his limbs with the golden trident, roaring in helpless fury, but it was no good. I tried to suck in air as my chest continued to tighten, dropping to my hands and starting to crawl toward Poseidon.

Atlas cackled loudly, and fire roared to life on the ground, rushing me. My whirlwind swept into my vision, blowing the flames out instantly. Fresh fire sprang up to replace it though.

I kept crawling, only one thought in my mind, my eyes locked on Poseidon's.

I knew what was happening to me.

This was the day all the prophecies would come true, it would seem.

Poseidon loved me.

And I loved him.

"Almi, please, no." Poseidon's voice reached me as I got closer, choking for air. My whirlwind was beating back Atlas and his fire, and a barrier of air was spinning around me, so fast it was clear.

The stone was spreading up Poseidon's waist now.

"I won't let you die." It was hard to get the words out, the invisible band squeezing my chest not allowing enough air into my body.

"Almi, run. Call Blue and run."

I drew on the immense power still coursing through me and dragged myself to my feet. "It's too late." I tried to smile, but the fear on his face was too much. "You offered your own life for hers."

"I would do anything for you."

"And I you. I love you."

Something snapped in his eyes, all the barely contained control leaving him completely. "This can not happen!" His voice was an anguished roar. "Take me! Take me and leave the nereids to live!"

I didn't know who he was yelling the plea at, but I couldn't stand the grief in his voice. I moved the last step toward him, pressing myself against the little flesh he had left, clasping my hands to his face.

"It wasn't supposed to happen like this. You and your sister were supposed to get the life I deprived you of." Regret and fear and bone-deep sorrow laced his tone as his wild eyes bore into mine. "It wasn't supposed to happen like this."

I gasped in a breath, before pressing my lips to his. "It's not your fault," I breathed, drawing back. "You did everything you could. The prophecy was clear. I'm going to die." I knew the pain in my chest was my oncoming death. But the sight of the man I had only just accepted that I loved turning into a godammned statue had filled me with an eerily calm, resolute rage. "If I'm going down, I'm taking them with me." If there was any chance at all that killing Medusa and Atlas would save Poseidon from the stone, then I was going to do everything I could to make it happen.

He shook his head, but I kissed him again. "I love you," I gasped against his lips. The words were like a balm, and I drew strength from them.

When he spoke them back, actual strength flowed through me, my spine straightening and my chest easing just a little. "I love you Almi. I always have."

I stepped back, and saw that the stone had almost reached his shoulders.

It was now or never.

# ALMI

*J*ust as I turned to Atlas, Kryvo's voice reached me. "Almi! Almi, the starfish on the font!"

Atlas fixed his hate-filled eyes on mine. Behind him, Ceto and Medusa were still locked in battle.

"It's too late, Kryvo. I'm so sorry."

"No! You must take me to the font! You must!"

He would be safer on the font, I realized, as Atlas began to advance toward me. I had no plan, as such. Just that I was going out with as big a bang as I could manage, and I was taking these fucking assholes with me. And I didn't want to do that with my friend attached to me.

Mustering my strength, I ran the few short steps to the font. I pulled Kryvo from my shoulder as I went, ready to set him onto the stone before Atlas could attack, but I faltered when I saw the fountain.

There were *hundreds* of starfish carved into the stone of the font.

I held my hand out to touch one, air magic swirling

around me and my shield expanding. As the air moved over the font, the starfish began to burst to life, just as Kryvo had. One by one, they peeled away from the stone and flew into the pool of water. The sounds of fighting fell away as I stared, my heart hammering.

Kryvo quivered in my hand. "You brought me to life," he squeaked. "I can feel your magic now, you brought me to life!"

He was right. I remembered how the air had blown in from the open bedroom window before he had come to life on my mirror.

A weird crashing realization filled me, knowledge that was coming from somewhere filled with magic drawing me to the truth.

"Kryvo, it's you," I whispered. My vision was swimming, and I could feel more and more magic building inside me. My chest burned with the pressure.

Somehow, I knew what I had to do. Magic compelled me, and I lifted the little starfish to my face as heat seared up my back. My air buffeted me, my magic warring with the Titan on my behalf behind me.

"Kryvo, you're going to save them all, you brave little starfish. You're the Heart of the Ocean."

Gently, I dropped him into the font with all the other starfish. The water pulsed, and I heard his voice in my head.

"Almi!"

"You're going to save Poseidon and all the people of Aquarius!" I told him again, watching as the water got brighter and brighter. I knew he would be safe. More than safe. He would become something new, something brilliant. "You're a hero, little Kryvo," I whispered.

Tears that I thought I had run out of sprang to my eyes again, and as the water got so bright it hurt, I turned back to Atlas.

I took as deep a breath as I could manage. I refused to look at Poseidon. I couldn't stand to see if the stone had taken him. Couldn't stand to tell him goodbye.

The Titan's furious eyes bore into mine, mania within them.

"Medusa!" I shouted as loud as my breathless body would allow. Atlas faltered at my summons, but behind me, I saw the two goddesses pause.

Ceto's voice rang in my mind. *You wish me to stop fighting her?*

*Yes.*

In a second, the woman was in front of me, standing beside her husband. I looked straight at her. The barrier of air between us would filter her deadly stare.

"You underestimated her, husband," she hissed to Atlas.

He snarled, and flames roared up around him. I felt the heat of the magic from the font behind me first, though, and then it began to flow around me, a thick tension building to a crescendo.

"What is happening? Why is the font—" Medusa's panicked words were cut off by a boom so deep it made the ground shake. Energy flowed from the font, and I held my arms out as it washed over me.

Healing energy.

It would do no good for me. The Heart of the Ocean

was never destined to save my life. But I turned my head, eyes misty with tears, and watched as the stone melted from Poseidon's body, rolling off his form like liquid.

A scream snapped my attention back ahead. The stone had left Lily's body too, pooling beneath her where she lay, then flowing across the ground. *Toward Medusa.* The stone that had left Poseidon was doing the same, and as it reached Medusa's feet it began to wind its way up her body.

"What's happening?" she shrieked, trying to move. Atlas scratched at the stone covering his wife's body, fury and fear on his face.

"You are being punished." Poseidon's voice rang out, and then he was beside me, pulling me tight against his body. Overpowering relief crashed over me, making me sag against him. I had failed to save Lily. But I had saved Poseidon. My air barrier expanded, encompassing him, too, and his trident gleamed gold. Water flowed from its tip into my air magic, making it gleam brighter silver.

"Make it stop!" Medusa screamed. Atlas turned to us, advancing a few steps then faltering, as though he didn't want to leave his wife.

"Make it stop, now!" he repeated, launching fire from his hands toward us.

The flames hit the water-wind wall of magic between us and petered out instantly.

"The font takes ill-will lethally," said Poseidon. "And your wife holds centuries of ill-will. Tell him the truth, Medusa. Clear your conscience, and the Underworld may treat you differently."

"I hate you!" she shrieked.

A new energy built around us, and as I looked at Atlas' terrified, maniacal face, I realized it was coming from him. All the warnings about the ancient Titan's strength washed over me, and fresh fear rose in me.

"Poseidon, you have to get out of here. Grab the red shell, and go," I said, turning into him.

He gripped my jaw, pressing a crushing kiss to my mouth before answering. "No. I will not leave you."

"I am dying, anyway. Please, live for both of us. And live the way you want, free and joyous."

He stared down at me, but the fear and sadness had gone. "I will fix this."

"Leave."

Medusa's frantic screams were increasing, so loud I only just heard Ceto in my head.

*My King, Queen, Atlas' power is becoming unstable. We need to leave.*

Medusa's screams cut off abruptly, and Atlas roared. I knew before I turned that she would be a statue.

"You will pay for this, ocean god!" Power hammered against our barrier, coming from every angle. I staggered, unable to take the attack, and the pressure in my chest magnified.

"Leave, Poseidon!" Ceto shouted. I was vaguely aware of her by the font, her hand hovering by the red shell. Kryvo floated above the fountain, only now he was covered in shining crystals and pearls.

Poseidon shouted as he launched power back at the Titan, and for the first time, I felt him as he should be.

The raw, colossal power of the ocean, unhindered by the stone blight. He was glorious.

Black swam in front of my eyes, and my throat closed tighter.

I slipped, and Poseidon pulled me upright.

"Let me go. Leave."

Heat swamped me, and I realized through my dizziness that we were surrounded by fire. My air magic was dying.

Poseidon bellowed, then water washed over me, making my already breathless chest work even harder.

"I love you." My legs crumpled as I gasped the words. More black crowded my vision; fire and water and the tang of power fading away as the pain flashed into agony. The excruciating feeling faded as quickly as it came, and a delicious serenity took me.

Then everything was gone.

# POSEIDON

"*H*ow does it feel, Poseidon? To watch your wife die?"

Atlas had not a drop of sanity left in him as he roared the words. I knew my own was teetering on the edge. I couldn't look at Almi's body on the ground beside me, or the little control that remained would flee me.

I knew what I needed to do. And I couldn't do it alone, not from the most inaccessible place in all of Olympus.

*Ceto, take the shell. End this.*

I couldn't win the Trials, nor could Almi. But he'd said Ceto and Kalypso were even on shells. And I needed the Trial over. I would have to take my chances with the sea goddess.

Power coursed through me, the feeling so welcome after such a long absence. I raised my trident high above my head.

"Creatures of the ocean, sea gods and goddesses of Olympus, hear my plea! This Titan wishes you ill! The Trials are over, and he must be dealt with!"

With an almighty push of power, I sent all my strength into the ocean beyond the dome around me. Atlas roared again, and Ceto launched inky black water at him as fire burst from his palms.

I cast my gaze up, feeling the response of the deep around me, answering my call. As I stared, creatures of all manner appeared beyond the glowing silver dome. Whales that had never seen daylight, twenty-feet long sea snakes and eels, fish of every size and shape, seals, dolphins, hippocampi, all swam alongside creatures many believed only existed in myth. Creatures as huge and terrifying as the talontaur, monsters that could only be seen by those who were guilty of horrific crimes, and deadly ocean wraiths arrived to aid me. When I saw the merfolk of the deep reach the dome, I knew that meant Ceto's brother, Phorkus, had answered my call. He was the god of the deep, and these creatures were his kin. Sure enough, I saw his inky, rotten form beyond the dome, shaped like his tentacled sister.

My trident grew hot in my hands as the hundreds of sea creatures kept flocking to the dome, to answer the call of their King. Light spewed from the tip of the trident, and as it hit the dome, everything shone gold.

"Rise!" I shouted the command, pouring my gloriously returned strength into the words. The creatures beyond the dome moved in a frenzy, and then the ground beneath my feet began to shake as the mass of creatures lent their strength in lifting Atlantis from the ocean floor.

We rose, slowly at first, then faster as more and more of my brethren answered my call. Kalypso appeared behind Atlas, and I prepared to call back some of my power to fight her, but she cast her eyes down to my feet where Almi's body lay, then back to mine. She nodded once, then shot jets of water from her palm at the scrabbling Atlas.

When daylight appeared above us, the sea animals began to dive away, the creatures of the deep unable to tolerate the light.

"Thank you. Your loyalty shall be honored," I boomed, then used my own power to raise Atlantis the rest of the way.

We burst through the surface, and I didn't need to send my next plea.

There was a series of flashing lights all around us, and as they cleared, I found myself surrounded by my kin.

Hades was beside me, Persephone to his left. Athena was to my right, and beyond her I saw the rest of the Olympians lined up opposite the insane Titan, with the exceptions of Zeus, Hera and Aphrodite.

"You broke the rules, Atlas," Athena said.

The Titan screamed, throwing his arm up and indicating the terrifying statue that used to be his wife. "He broke the rules! Centuries ago, he tried to defile my wife!"

"No. The Font of Zoi is older than all of us. Its magic is beyond question. *It* deemed her unworthy. The monster Medusa became was a representation of her true nature. She did that, not Poseidon." Athena's voice rang with melodic wisdom.

"Lies!" With a searing burst of heat, Kalypso's water and Ceto's inky ribbons disintegrated.

No words needed to be exchanged between me and

my brother. In unison, Hades and I launched power at the Titan. Athena, Ares, Apollo, and Artemis added streams of glowing magic to ours, and Atlas screamed in pain. Hephaestus, then Dionysus, then Hermes added their own power, and Atlas rose from the ground.

"To Tartarus?" growled Hades. He was in his smoke form, huge and oozing terror that would have sent a mortal mad.

"To Tartarus," I agreed. As one, we focused out power. I pictured the horrific fiery pit of hell that was the underworld prison, Tartarus. Hades rose from the ground too, his bright blue power swirling with light. Bodies formed from the light, an army of corpses, ready to take their prisoner. Athena called out a battle cry, and I poured every drop of power I had into the stream wrapping around Atlas. He shrieked as Hades' army swamped him. There was a flash of blue light, and the god of the dead vanished, along with Atlas.

"Poseidon, she's… she's…." Persephone was on her knees, her golden vines wrapped around Almi's form. Her eyes were filled with tears, and her voice shook. "She's dead."

"Not for long," I growled. I bent, scooping my wife up in my arms. Persephone's vines vanished immediately, and I swallowed down bile at the feeling of Almi's cold, lifeless skin.

"Brethren. Will you bring her back?"

Athena looked at me sadly. "Without Zeus, we can not.

All the Olympian gods are needed for this feat. I am sorry, Poseidon."

I turned away from the goddess.

"Zoi! Behold the last of the Nereids! You save species from extinction, and the Nereids are worth saving. I beseech you!" My voice broke on the last sentence, and I lay Almi down in front of the font. Her starfish, encrusted in jewels and hovering over the font, pulsed with light.

"Poseidon, if the font doesn't deem her worthy, she may return a monster."

I ignored Athena.

"Kryvo. Tell me what to do."

I heard the starfish's tiny voice in my head. *Give her water.*

I leaned forward, scooping water up from the font in my hands. I knelt carefully and looked at her face for the first time since the life at left her.

I couldn't bear it. Anguish beyond anything I had ever known made my chest feel like it was shattering.

*Give her the water.* Kryvo's voice seeped through the pain. I bent over her and tipped the water from the font over her colorless lips.

Nothing happened. Silence dominated. Absolutely nothing happened.

Then the ocean breeze gusted over us, a tiny whirlwind appearing beside me. It danced toward Almi's face and as it reached the droplets of water running uselessly down her face, it gathered them up, and made a miniature whirlpool of air and water.

Carefully, delicately, it moved to her tattoo. I watched, my breath held, as it appeared to melt into her skin. The center of the shell tattoo flared with life and color, vivid green. I didn't dare release my breath as the color swirled out, filling the shell, and then rippled over the rest of her skin. The pallid tone faded, lively pink replacing it. Then her chest moved, her lungs filling. She gasped, and her eyes flickered open.

# ALMI

*L*ight pricked at the darkness.

"What..." I tried to say, but my throat didn't work. I wasn't breathing, I realized abruptly. Panic swamped me as I tried to orient myself, tried to open my eyes or make my chest work. With a rush, I felt air flow down my throat and fill my lungs. My eyelids cracked open, and through the haze, I saw Poseidon.

Memories crashed through me as I stared up at his face.

*His smile.*

That devastating smile was stretched across his face, and then his hand was on my cheek, brushing my hair back.

"Almi," he breathed.

My head pounded, and my vision was blurry.

"What..." I tried again, but air whooshed over my face, and a little whirlwind came into focus.

Something stirred in my gut, alien and raw and not

unpleasant. The whirlwind expanded, whizzing around me, and Poseidon's smile slipped.

"What are you doing?" he barked, his fingers tightening around my shoulders. I was vaguely aware that I was lying on the ground, but then the whirlwind tightened around me and pulled me from Poseidon's grasp. He cried out and Persephone appeared beside him as I was lifted higher into the air. She said something to him, and a jet of water burst from his palm toward the whirlwind. The pain and disorientation was leaving me, the feeling in my gut spreading through me instead.

*I was supposed to be dead.*

The realization hammered into me as I stared down into Poseidon's confused face.

*I had died.*

How was I back?

I felt something warm and slightly sharp against my hand and looked down.

"Kryvo." He was beautiful.

"He saved you," the little starfish said gleefully, as an image of Poseidon calling all of the creatures of the sea burst to life behind my eyelids. I watched as Atlantis rose from the ocean, and the Olympians arrived and cast Atlas into Tartarus.

Numbness still suffocated my mind, even as I felt the power building inside me. I watched as Poseidon lifted my body, and carried me to the font.

"He brought me back," I murmured.

"The font brought you back. It deemed you worthy."

I opened my eyes, dispelling the vision. "What's happening now?"

"You are being reborn with the Heart of the Ocean."

"That's you?"

"Yes."

"I don't understand."

"I belong to you. You have my power now, as well as your own."

"Your power?"

"Yes. Immortality. You're a goddess now, Almi." I could hear the glee in his voice.

The whirlwind around us spun even faster, and I tried to get my brain to catch up as I hovered within it. "A goddess?"

"Yes. Embrace it."

As he said the words, the air stopped spinning. For a second I thought I would plummet to the floor, but a torrent of magic exploded inside me, and the whole world froze.

That same weird, expanding knowledge I'd had in front of the font filled me. I could be anywhere I wanted, instantly. And I knew exactly where that was.

I flashed, right into Poseidon's arms.

"You're back." He gripped my face, kissing me everywhere. I laughed, pushing at his chest.

"I'm back. And Kryvo says I'm a goddess now."

"Almi!"

I turned at Persephone's voice. One by one, the other Olympians were disappearing in flashes of light, but my attention went to where my friend was kneeling on the ground. Next to Lily.

I moved quickly, Poseidon still clutching my hand. Persephone beamed up at me as I reached them. "Almi, look."

I followed her pointing hand to my sister. A tiny spinning whirlwind flecked with drops of water sank into the shell tattoo on her chest.

And then her ribs moved.

I dropped to my knees, putting my hand to her cheek. She was warm. Her skin was the right color.

Excitement thrilled through me, disbelief hot on its heels.

"Almi?" Lily's eyes opened slowly as she said my name.

"I'm here, Lily. I'm here." Tears of joy spilled down my cheeks, as I looked into her bright blue eyes. "We're all here."

I was scared that I was actually dead, and this was all some weird afterlife dream or something.

My sister was alive. And awake. Staring up at me, a weak smile on her lips.

"You asked the font to save the last of the Nereids. It has brought them both back," Persephone breathed through her smile, her healing vines wrapping around Lily's wrists. "She needs water."

Water flowed from Poseidon's glowing hand, precise and gentle as it reached Lily's lips. His power felt different now, and I remembered what he'd said about me being a beacon to him. I felt drawn to it, like it had its own life and sound, and it was calling to me.

As if hearing my thoughts, a stream of water broke away, making its way to me instead. I held my hand out, and a trickle of air flowed from me. When the two met, silver light glowed, and the stream of water and air intertwined with each other, dancing before us.

A sense of utter rightness settled over me. This was happening. This was real.

*"I love you."*

The words were in my head, in Poseidon's deep, beautiful voice. I turned my face from Lily, who was still drinking, to look at him.

"I love you," I whispered. "This is real, right?"

Kryvo squeaked from where I'd hurriedly pressed him to my collar. "One hundred percent real. Look, it's Blue and Chrysos."

I snapped my head left to see the two pegasi galloping into the clearing. Blue didn't stop until he reached me, and I stroked his nose, peppering his long snout with kisses.

"Boy, am I glad you're safe," I told him. Tears were burning at the backs of my eyes, but this time through sheer joy.

"I know this is an emotional time for you all," Athena's voice rang out through the clearing. "But there is the matter of the Poseidon Trials to settle."

Poseidon stiffened beside me, and I focused on the goddess. Ceto was next to her, tentacles squelching on the ground. An uneasy feeling washed over me.

We may have been saved, but Poseidon might have lost his realm.

"Ceto won the most shells. As per the rules of the

Trials, she is entitled to reign over Aquarius." Athena's voice was tight and reluctant. Ceto's gaze fell on Poseidon.

"I am willing to make a deal, sea king."

He bowed to her, still not releasing my hand. "I am grateful. And I have a worthy offer."

She inclined her head at him. "You owe me, Poseidon. I will only consider a grand offer."

"How would you like to rule Atlantis?"

I looked at him in surprise, then back at Ceto. She blinked slowly. "You offer me a city in ruins?" Her words were unimpressed, but her tone belied an undercurrent of what I was sure was excitement.

"Yes. I would like to offer the inhabitants citizenship in Aquarius, should they wish to take it-" he started, but I gripped his arm, cutting him off.

"The inhabitants?"

He beamed down at me, and my knees felt weak. "Yes. They are all alive. I can feel them."

Joy rushed me, and I bounced on my feet involuntarily. "And the victims in Aquarius?"

"We are too far from them for me to tell, but if the ancient people here have been cured, then I think it is, for once, safe to get our hopes up." His face was alive with emotion.

"You offer me a city in ruins, with no population?" Ceto called, drawing both of our attentions back to her.

"Indeed. A city with power. A city with one of the most ancient and powerful artifacts of Olympus in it."

"Poseidon," Athena said, worry in her voice. "The Font of Zoi must be protected. It must never be abused."

Poseidon kept his eyes locked on Ceto. "This goddess is trustworthy. I will vouch for her. She has been a part of the creation of many creatures of the sea, and she cares for them as her own. She deals in respect. There would be no better guardian for the font's power."

"Very well," Athena said. "You are responsible for this decision, Poseidon."

"Will you take Atlantis, in return for me keeping Aquarius?" Poseidon said to Ceto.

She was silent a long moment. "Can you return the city to the bottom of the ocean?"

"Yes."

"Then yes. I accept your offer." Ceto's voice rang in my mind, straight after her spoken words. *The debt is clear, sea King, Queen.*

With a flash, she vanished. Athena gave Poseidon a piercing look, then she vanished too.

Polybotes stamped up to take her place. He was completely free of stone, and must have stayed out of the fighting once he had been brought back. Given that he had no magic, I couldn't blame him. He fixed his huge eyes on me. "You have saved my life twice. You have my allegiance." He looked at Poseidon. "You are an asshole, and I will only abandon my revenge because your wife is better than you." With a nod, he stamped away, disappearing into the maze. I looked up at Poseidon, eyebrows raised and a grin on my lips.

"You're going to have to tell me the story with you two." He started to answer, but Lily's voice reached me.

"Almi." I dropped to my knees. Persephone's vines

were still around her, and I glanced at my friend. "Is she okay?"

"I'm fine," Lily answered for herself. Persephone nodded at me, beaming.

"Lily." I leaned forward, wrapping my arms tightly around her, pulling her into a sitting position. She returned my hug fiercely.

"I told you so." Her lips were cracked, and her voice was scratchy, but she was grinning at me as I moved back to look at her.

"You told me what?"

"All of it! That you would get your power and be stronger than me. That you would save the world. That the god of the sea was in love with you." She cast a playful glance up at Poseidon.

"It really was you talking to me all that time." Happy tears crept down my cheeks.

"Of course it was. I never left you."

"I love you, Lily."

"I know. I love you too."

# ALMI

"Do I have to do this?" The little nymph straightened the hem of my dress as my sister laughed.

"Yes. You do."

"In front of all those people?"

"That's kind of the point. Turn around so I can see you."

I shuffled around on the little podium I was standing on so that Lily could see me. Her eyes lit up, and she moved so that I could see the full-length mirror behind her.

My reflection stared back, and I never would have believed I could look like I did. The vividly bright shell tattoo, the shining, mother-of-pearl skin tone and the bright blue and silver-streaked hair were one thing. But the wedding dress?

Never in a million years did I expect that.

.  .  .

It was the palest of greens, with silver and blue—to match my hair—shimmering in the fabric. The top was a stiff corset with completely sheer sleeves that draped low down my arms like liquid. The skirt flowed over my hips, glittering with the hint of bright rolling clouds and cresting waves when I moved.

It was a stunning dress. I looked at Lilly, who had tears in her eyes.

"What's wrong?"

"You look amazing. And I never thought I would see you again, let alone be here with you when you marry the man you love."

"Oh, Lily. I'm so glad you're here too." The nymph moved back, allowing me to step down from the pedestal and gather Lily into a hug.

It had only been two nights since the showdown in Atlantis, and Lily and I had been inseparable since.

Poseidon had been completely occupied in handing Atlantis over to Ceto, moving the citizens into his own realm, and then sinking it back to the bottom of the ocean. Along with Persephone, Lily and I had been helping all the people who had been afflicted by the stone blight, and it turned out that my new magic made me the perfect person for the job. Or perfect *goddess* for the job. I glanced at the little jewel-encrusted starfish sitting on a cushion on the dresser.

Kryvo was the Heart of the Ocean, and his power was mine. And it seemed he wasn't just immortal. He had telepathic powers. Which meant, so did I. With a little guidance from Persephone, I was able to help adjust the memories of those families who had lost loved ones to the stone, so that they never knew anything so serious had ever occurred.

It was satisfying work, and it made me truly happy to help put all the broken families back together again, my own sister and friend alongside me.

But it had only taken hours of being back in Aquarius for me to start missing the sea king. Within a day of not seeing him, I started to feel... wrong. Twitchy and uncharacteristically melancholy.

The lack of his presence made me unable to think straight, or even eat properly. All I could think about, all I wanted, was him.

Then a note had appeared under my door.

Not a note, an invitation. To my own wedding.

*Poseidon, King of the Ocean, invites you to witness his formal bonding to Almi, Nereid and Queen of Aquarius. The event will also serve as her official coronation. Regards.*

There was a scrawled signature at the bottom that was totally illegible.

I had stared at the piece of paper, confusion and a touch of anger welling up inside me, until Lily had taken it from me, and after reading it, turned it over.

There was a sketch on the back, of my shell. It was beautifully done, and it made my breath catch. And in handwritten script beneath was a single sentence. A question.

*Will you become my Queen, before my realm?*

Galatea had arrived the next morning to say the ceremony would take place immediately and that Roz and Mav would be waiting in the dressing room with my dress.

"You'll need a garter," said Lily, putting her hand on her chin and looking me up and down.

I was about to protest that that was old-fashioned and a human thing, but then a thought struck me. "The blindfold."

"What?"

"The piece of his toga he cut for me, to blindfold my eyes."

"Great idea. I'll go get it."

Lily scurried off to find it, and I took a deep breath as I looked at my reflection again. My longing for Poseidon had become as physical as it had emotional. I was connected to him as deeply as if we shared a beating heart.

I understood the need for the ceremony. Both Lily and Galatea had made the point that if I was now a goddess and recognized as Poseidon's wife, then it needed to be made official to the people of his realm, as well as to the other gods.

But I didn't need all this over-the-top nonsense. I just needed him.

I would sacrifice anything I owned to see that smile on

his face. To feel his warm skin against mine, free of cold hard granite. To feel his powerful aura washing over me, to hear his whoop of joy as we soared through the air and the ocean together.

A small noise escaped my lips as I screwed my face up with impatience.

I wanted him here, beside me, now.

The one good thing about having a formal wedding, I thought as I stared at my skirt in the mirror, was that weddings were followed by *wedding nights*.

My dreams had become more intense, and I knew that I was far, far more excited — and nervous — about the evening than the wedding vows or wearing a crown.

I would finally feel the way Poseidon's desire-filled eyes, husky voice and tense body had promised I would. He would be able to do anything he liked to me. I would let him. Anticipation sent thrills across my skin.

"Aquarius will be lucky to have such a beautiful Queen." I saw Galatea standing behind me in the mirror, and I forced the filthy thoughts from my mind. I smiled as I turned to her.

"Thank you. I'm glad you think so."

"I do. Are you ready?"

Lily burst back into the room, holding the strip of fabric triumphantly.

I took a deep breath. "I am now."

The ceremony was held in the throne room, and Persephone was waiting for me outside the door when we ascended the stairs.

"Wow. You look… like a goddess."

"I feel like one," I grinned.

"Hey, Kryvo, way to go saving the day," she said to the starfish, who was adorning my wrist like a big sparkly corsage.

He heated on my skin. "Thanks," he squeaked happily.

"Who would have guessed he would be the Heart of the Ocean?"

"I certainly didn't," I said. "I didn't even know I'd brought him to life. I thought he was part of the palace's magic."

"I didn't know either," the starfish said. "I didn't become what I was meant to be until you embraced your power," he said.

"Fascinating," said Persephone, eyes gleaming with interested excitement. She was wearing a stunning yellow and green dress, covered in black lace made up of roses. Her white hair was braided, and she wore a golden tiara shaped from thorns. "You know, I'd love to study him, see if I can work out how you brought him to life," she said to me.

"I, erm, won't be needing his company tonight," I said awkwardly, feeling my face heat. "Kryvo, do you want to stay with Persephone this evening?"

"I would rather be anywhere than with you and Poseidon tonight," he said.

Persephone laughed. "That settles it then." She looked at Lily standing next to me, wearing a stunning flowing gown of rich sparkling teal, that complimented her hair perfectly. "How are you feeling?"

My sister and my new friend had gotten along great the last few days, and it made my heart sing to be with them both.

"Excited to see my little sister get married. Properly this time," grinned Lily.

"That makes one of us," I mumbled.

Persephone raised her eyebrows. "You don't want to marry him?" She looked at the huge, gilded doors behind her. "It's a bit late to back out now. They're all waiting for you in there."

I shook my head. "No, it's just, I don't usually deal with all this…" I swept my arm out. "Formality. And drama."

"You just participated in the Poseidon Trials, which were shown to the whole of Olympus. I think you're fairly embedded in the drama."

"Hmm."

"You need to give your adoring audience their happy ending," smiled Lily. "And anyway, you love him. Go and enjoy telling the world that."

As she said the words, I realized that that was exactly where my hang-up was.

I had to tell him I loved him and was choosing to be his wife, in front of the whole world. But I hadn't even told *him* that.

Well, I had told him I loved him. Me dropping dead was all the evidence he had needed that the love was real and mutual. But, other than in the chaos that was the last trial, we hadn't had a single moment to actually say the words or work out what they meant to us.

Declaring this newfound love in front of a load of strangers was bound to feel a little uncomfortable.

I nodded at my sister. "Okay. Let's do this."

The gilded doors eased open, and I linked my arm in Lily's and followed Persephone into the throne room.

# ALMI

*W*aiting for Almi to enter the room, waiting to lay eyes on her beautiful face, was going to kill me. Immortal or not, it might actually kill me.

I had refrained from even speaking with her as I cleared up the mess Atlas had left behind, because I knew that I would not be able to maintain my control if given even the slightest temptation. And just her voice, her words, her wit… Speaking with her would have been enough for me to abandon all of my duties, whisk her away to my ship, and spend as much time as I needed to wipe away a decade of resentment and pain.

So instead, I had focused everything I had on doing what needed to be done, and subsequently, the last two days had felt as long as the last eight years. Because now, I knew she loved me back. I could feel it, an invisible cord between us, thrumming with life and hope and love.

She gave me an energy that was boundless, her presence cajoling and freeing, a feisty mass of all the things I had missed so sorely from my long, serious life.

Fuck, I had missed her. I wanted her, *needed* her by my side. After the cursed formality of the vows and coronation were out of the way, the world would not see us for far more than two days, I would make sure of that.

The throne from my throne room was gone, an altar and priestess of Hera replacing it. A large, peacock headdress denoted the slight woman as such, and I noticed she was smiling at the back of the room. Gods and goddesses lined the walls of the room, including my brother, but none caught my attention as I turned.

The doors were open. Persephone glided into the room, beaming. She swept to one side, to stand in place next to Hades, and there, arm in arm with her sister, was Almi.

I had thought that when I saw her, the tension that had plagued my body would lessen. But the opposite was true.

She looked beyond beautiful. Radiant. The Goddess, and Queen, that she always should have been.

My whole body stiffened, and warmth flooded me. When her gaze met mine, I saw my own smile reflected back at me, sincere joy on her face. And desire in her eyes.

Her sister kissed her cheek when she reached me, then moved to stand with Persephone. Almi looked up at me, her expression almost shy. I took her hand, then nodded at the priest to start the ceremony.

*You look stunning.*

Her mouth twitched as the priestess spoke about eternal bonds and lifelong commitments. *You don't look too bad yourself. Now shh, I'm listening.*

*We've heard them once before.*

She narrowed her eyes at me. *I wasn't really listening then, either.*

Regretting bringing up the past, I tried to focus on the priestess. But all I could pay attention to was her. The silver streaks shone in her hair, and her skin glowed. She smelled like the breeze on the ocean.

*I missed you.*

Her voice sounded in my mind, and happiness coursed through my veins.

*I missed you too. More every minute.*

*Why didn't you talk to me then? Or come and see me?*

*Because I do not have the self-control required not to have abandoned my duties and taken you far away from all this. Somewhere we can enjoy each other at our long leisure.*

Her cheeks pinked, and I could see the need in her, as strong and fierce as my own.

*How long is this thing?*

I grinned at her, just as the priestess said, "With this crown…" Galatea stepped toward us. She was holding a cushion, and on it was a crown I'd never believed would adorn any head.

It was dainty, made from seashells and coral, with tiny gemstones set throughout that made it sparkle. I had found time before the ceremony to alter it a little, carving tiny whirlwinds into the three larger shells. Almi reached for it, eyes wide with wonder. She brushed a finger over one of the carvings.

"You carved this?" It was a question, but she already knew the answer.

I nodded. "Yes. You are not of the ocean. But you belong with it. That should be celebrated."

She beamed at me, and I took the crown from her, placing it gently on her head. The crowd clapped and roared, her friend from the bakery louder than all of the others.

The priestess spoke again. "And now, before Olympus, you must affirm your love for one another. Almi, do you assent to the bonding of your soul to Poseidon?"

She looked at me, those bright, determined eyes full of certainty. And joy. "I do."

"And Poseidon, do you assent to the bonding of your soul to Almi?"

"I do." With the words came a release of guilt I hadn't realized had been weighing so hard on me. A sense of freedom washed over me, raising the hairs on my arms and sending tingling sensations across my body. I knew Almi felt it too, because she gave a tiny gasp and gripped my hands.

"By the magic of Hera, you are wed and bound," said the priestess.

I lifted Almi's hand as I turned to the assembled room. "Aquarius, I present to you your Queen."

# ALMI

*an we leave yet?* I sent the telepathic thought to Poseidon as yet another person I didn't recognize bowed before us, extending their heartfelt congratulations on our wedding.

*Soon, my love.*

I gave a sigh, covering it quickly with a cough as our admirer bade his farewells. Poseidon gave me a sideways smile, loaded with promise.

*You've waited a long time. A few hours won't make any difference.*

"Hours!" I exclaimed aloud. His smile widened.

My body had come alive the second I'd seen him at the altar, all my annoyance and reticence vanishing in a flash. There was nothing in Olympus I wanted more than to show him how much he meant to me. And to feel the same from him.

He was right, I had waited a long time. My whole damn adult life, I'd been waiting to find out what a man would feel like inside me. And it turned out I'd waited for exactly the right reason.

Him.

I was ready, and I was done waiting.

If I was a Queen now, I was damn well going to act like one.

I glared at him, my mental words brooking no argument. Husband, take me to bed. Now.

His eyelids dipped, bright blue eyes darkening. How can I refuse a command from her majesty? he said, and the world flashed.

When I blinked, we were in the bedroom on his ship. The huge, shell-shaped bed, covered in black silk stood beckoning us.

Before I could say a word, he pulled me tight against him, both his hands on my face. He drew his thumbs down my cheeks as he stared into my eyes.

"Alone, at last," he breathed.

Heat swept my body, pooling between my legs.

This was happening.

"You are so very, very beautiful."

I wetted my lips, drawing in a breath. "As are you, my king." He flashed me a devastating grin, and I bit my lip. "That smile makes me weak. I can't believe you hid it for so long."

"I can't believe I haven't been able to do this for so long," he replied, before dipping his head and pressing his lips to mine.

It started as a gentle kiss, fitting of two people in love. But as his tongue parted my lips, and the taste of him flooded my senses, it turned into an entirely different kind of kiss. A kiss that showed me how much he wanted me.

A kiss that touched every part of me.

A kiss that made my knees buckle.

He scooped me up, holding me close as he moved us to the bed. All I could do was hold onto him. My mind reeled with the sensation of his body pressed against mine. The heat of his mouth, the smoothness of his skin, the hardness of his body.

He lowered me to the bed, his lips never leaving mine the whole time. When my back came into contact with the sheets, he pulled away, only to rain kisses down my neck. He bit down gently, teeth grazing my skin and making me tingle everywhere.

"You are so soft," he murmured. "I want to hear you scream."

I took a shaky breath, letting the need that his words had created spread through me, willing myself to relax. He moved back, and when he looked down into my eyes, I could see the impatience and desire warring on his face. I reached up and cupped his cheek.

Feeling bold, I moved to my knees slowly, gripping his shoulders. "Help me with my corset?"

Before he could answer, I turned my back to him. I felt his fingers on the laced-up back of my dress, firm but gentle as he untied and loosened the ribbon.

When I felt the heavy fabric was loose enough, I took a deep breath and lifted my arms straight above my head. There was a pause, and my dress slid up my body.

He was tall enough that he had no problem removing it, leaving me kneeling in nothing but lace panties and my blindfold garter. Terrified at my nakedness, and desperate to see his nakedness, I turned slowly to face him, dropping my arms back to my sides.

He hissed in a breath, his eyes blazing as they took in my breasts, my belly, my panties.

I dropped my eyes deliberately to his toga-clad waist. In a movement almost too fast to follow, he rid himself of it.

I couldn't help my gasp.

Every inch of him was hard, sculpted muscle.

Every inch.

He was magnificent. Solid muscles covered his chest, with just a dusting of hair leading down south to the soft-looking skin I'd stroked before. My eyes dropped lower, and I moaned. He was already hard, his cock bobbing before me, long and thick and perfect.

I couldn't help reaching out. He twitched, and I thought he was going to stop me, but then he stilled. I wrapped my fingers around his shaft and looked up at him.

He gave a growl that was pure satisfaction as his gaze bored into mine. I turned my face and licked the tip of his cock.

He growled again, his body tensing. I licked the tip again, and then swirled my tongue around it. He tasted salty and warm, and I liked it. I took him deep in my mouth, sucking softly. His hands gripped my hair, and he spoke breathlessly. "My queen." His cock swelled even bigger against my tongue and his hands tightened in my hair. I grasped his cock firmly and sucked, working my tongue and mouth on him. I felt him shudder, then heard him groan and felt him shudder again. "Stop."

He pulled away, and I gasped, licking my lips and staring up at him as he took a ragged breath.

"I've waited so long for you," he growled.

"And I you," I breathed, my voice hitched. Desire was pulsing through me, so intense it was almost unbearable. "Touch me," I whispered.

"Take off your panties," he commanded.

I felt a fresh rush of heat at his command, and I obeyed, pulling down my white lace panties.

The instant I was uncovered, he was on me.

He picked me up, my legs wrapping around his waist as he pressed me against the sheets. My back sank into the black silk, his weight crushing me into the covers. My nipples brushed against the hard wall of his chest, and I arched into him.

The feel of his skin against mine was electric. His hand moved between us, stroking down my belly as he took my mouth in a fierce kiss. His finger found my wetness and I moaned into his lips.

"You are ready for me." It was a question and a statement together, and he sounded as close to edge as I felt.

"So ready. I love you."

He stilled his stroking, lifting his head from mine to stare at me. "I love you."

He shifted as he said the words, and I felt his cock against my entrance. I bit my lip. "You are mine, now and forever. And I yours."

"Forever."

Gently, so gently, he pressed into me, dropping his lips to mine again.

I sucked in a gasp at the feeling, and he moved, kissing my jaw and my neck. He stretched me, a slight discomfort taking me as he moved deeper. But the pain vanished quickly, and he withdrew a little.

"Okay?" He asked against my skin.

"Yes."

"More?"

"More."

He pressed even deeper into me, and I cried out. He held himself there, even as he covered my jaw in more kisses. "Good?"

"Good," I panted.

"More?"

"There's more?" He nipped at my neck and pressed even further into me. I let out a long moan, and he wound an arm under me, pulling me tight against him. I arched into it, letting the feeling of fullness take me.

He began to move. My gasps turned into moans as he withdrew before slowly pressing back in. Again and again, he moved, taking me slowly, and my arms wound around his shoulders. My eyes closed in pleasure, and I lost myself in the feeling of him buried deep inside me. I felt him shudder against me, his body tensing.

I lifted my head and kissed him hard on the mouth. He groaned, and I felt him shudder again. He moved faster, and I wrapped my legs tighter around him, my arms pulling him closer. He kissed me, deeply, fiercely, his tongue possessing mine.

I was close. I felt it building, the tingling starting in my belly as he moved inside me. My body felt like it was on fire, and I was starting to feel lightheaded, but each thrust of his body filling me was pure pleasure. I moaned into his mouth.

"Come for me," he breathed.

I shook, my body quaking as my orgasm exploded through me, pleasure bursting through me in waves. Lights flashed behind my closed eyelids, and I was only vaguely aware of the cry I had made. Poseidon growled as I clenched around him, and he moved faster. My body burned with the intensity of my climax, and I was still clinging to the edge when he groaned and pushed deep into me, shuddering as he came.

His cock twitched, and again, and again, filling me with warmth. He collapsed on top of me, and I welcomed the feeling of his weight on me.

He kissed me, sweet, gentle kisses as he held me against him.

"Mine," he murmured, his voice deep and satisfied.

"Always."

We lay like that for a long time, my face against his chest, my arms around his shoulders, him still buried deep inside me.

"I believe I said I wanted you to scream," he said eventually.

He lifted himself up on his elbows, and I looked up at him. He kissed me softly.

"Did I not scream?"

"You definitely made some noise," he said, eyes burning. "But nothing I would qualify as a scream." He moved inside me, slowly but solidly.

"I don't know," I said breathlessly. "I'm pretty sure I screamed when I came."

He shook his head. "No, my love. What you call a scream, I call a moan."

He brought his face down to mine and kissed me, his hips stilling. I whimpered at the loss of him, and he said against my lips, "Ah, you see? There it is."

He moved again, his cock sliding in and out of me slowly, steadily. I shivered at the sensation still sparking within me, and I looked up at him, biting my lip. "I want to come again."

He grinned at me. I squeaked as he scooped an arm underneath me and rolled. When we came to a stop, he was on his back, and I was on top.

Gently, he put a hand flat on my middle and pushed me back so that I was straddling him. His eyes devoured my breasts hungrily.

Pushing up onto his elbows, he moved his lips to my hard nipple. I closed my eyes, letting the sensation wash over me, the intensity of the pleasure of his tongue with the un-ignorable feeling of his cock still filling me. I ground my hips, pressing myself onto him hard. He growled against my skin, before moving to my other nipple.

I ground harder, the feeling delicious.

He lay back, staring up at me. His look took my breath away. For the first time, I felt like a really could be a goddess and a queen.

Then his thumb found my clit, and all thoughts abandoned me. He lifted his hips, bouncing me on his hardness, whilst his soft, clever hands worked some sort of magic. The dual sensations were too much, especially off the back of such an intense orgasm.

I cried out, and he froze.

My eyelids flew open.

He smiled at me, then gripped my ass with his other hand. Pulling me forward, then pushing me back, he made me ride his length, stroking me at the same time.

I felt myself tighten around him, pressure building inside me, dizzying and uncontainable.

"Let go. And remember to scream."

I did.

I screamed his name as my orgasm ripped through me, my body shaking. His hand dug into my ass, pulling me down onto him hard, then he thrust into me, hard and fast, his hands pulling my hips down onto him.

He gasped, then growled as he came, pumping his hot, thick release into me.

Him filling me pushed me even higher, and I let out a long whimper, my entire body alive with sensation.

I fell forward, collapsing onto his solid chest, and his hands played up and down my bare back as he breathed heavily.

"That was definitely a scream," he said, his voice thick with satisfaction.

I smiled at him, then let my head fall back to his chest. My eyes closed as exquisite contentment took me.

Everything was right. For the first time in my life, everything was right.

. . .

I started to drift off, and I snuggled into him. His arms wrapped tightly around me, and he kissed me gently on the forehead.

"This is where you belong, Queen Almi. With me. Always."

"And where you belong is in the skies and the ocean, not in a stuffy throne room," I murmured against his chest. "You and I are going to have some fun, Mr. King."

He chuckled, and the sound made me beam. "If you're by my side, I'll do whatever I'm bid. I love you."

"I love you, too. Always."

# THANKS FOR READING!

Thank you so much for reading The Poseidon Trials! If you enjoyed Almi and Poseidon's story, I would be so grateful for a review.

If you've read my previous series (Olympus Academy particularly) you may have noticed that I have a small obsession with the ocean. I am a scuba diver and have been lucky enough to experience some incredible encounters with marine life around the world (along with my fiercely adventurous mother) and the raw power and insanely massive wealth of life in the sea makes me feel a kind of way nothing else does. So, needless to say, I've wanted to write Poseidon's story for a really long time :)

I hope I did it justice! I enjoyed writing this series so much. A lot of my favorite parts of the story came to me as I wrote them (I'm looking at you, Kryvo), which is always so exciting as the author, because you kind of get to experience it as the reader might.

I also found myself calling my husband crying whilst writing this last book, which is a first. It turns out I'm really bad at killing my characters!!

I want to extend a heartfelt thank you to you, for reading my books. I'm writing every day now, and that's because amazing people like you are supporting your favorite authors by buying their books.

YOU ARE AMAZING.

## WHAT'S NEXT...

I will be making a short departure from Olympus for my next series, but there will still be plenty of mythology, magic and, of course, romance, involved. Along with some seriously manly viking heroes...

You can get exclusive access to cut scenes and first looks at artwork and story ideas, plus free short stories and audiobooks if you sign up to my newsletter at elizaraine.com and you can hang out with me and get teasers, giveaways and release updates (and pictures of my pets) by joining my Facebook reader group, just search for Eliza Raine Author!

# ACKNOWLEDGMENTS

Thank you so much to my editor Dayna, who has been amazing at dealing with my complete inability to work with deadlines and always makes my stories stronger.

Thank you so much to my author friends, Simone especially, for constantly motivating me and helping me talk out all those parts that don't make sense. You've made writing this series so freaking enjoyable.

And thank you to my husband and mum, for dealing with my perpetual nonsense!!! I love you xxx

Made in United States
Orlando, FL
25 July 2022

20162070R00145